THIS GAME CALLED *Life*

MARIE A. NORFLEET

THIS
GAME
CALLED
Life

Dedications

First and foremost, I want to thank my Lord and Savior for giving me the strength and allowing me the time and energy to write this story. I give all glory and praise unto him because He is a merciful God and a forgiving God. He has taken hold of my life and guided me to the path He set for me, not the path I was choosing for myself.

I would like to dedicate this book to my children: Antwoine, Maurice, Noel and Makayla.

Mommy loves y'all more than life itself. All that I do, is done for y'all. Let Mommy's struggles and her prevail be the inspiration y'all need to always push forward in life.

To My Mother Sharonnda

I want to thank you for giving me that tough love when I needed it and keeping it real when I couldn't tell the difference. Because of you, I am the woman I am today, a woman of whom you can be proud of. Thank you for the countless hours you spent, grinding at work just to give me and my brothers a comfortable life. Most of all, thank you for being my mother, thank you for the life lessons and values that I now pass on to my children. I love you!

I also would like to dedicate this book to my grandfather, Lewis Charles Johnson.

This journey hasn't always been an easy one but I'm glad I had you through most of the hard parts. Now that you're gone, it won't be the same but I will push on. I hope I make you proud!

I'll be missing you forever and a day…until I see you again!!!

Rest In Peace Grandpa Charles

I Love You, B.A.M

Acknowledgements

I would like to thank the following book clubs and their administrators for accepting me into their groups without hesitation, for allowing me the opportunity to promote my book, for advertising it for me at times, and for the positive feedback and interactions.

The Black Faithful Sisters and Brothers Book Club (Carla, Zaneta, and Gabrielle)

My Urban Book Club (Mary Green)

Nook and Kindle Readers

Nook Readers

Extended Sisters Book Club (Shawnda Hamilton)

There is a long list but I want to name a few of the ladies who have been holding it down from the beginning;

Hadiya McDuffie, Brandy aka Bunfaithful, Lisa Wells, Dwana Boochie and Mildred Garrett

Thank you ladies for the continuous love and support!!!

THIS GAME CALLED *Life*

CHAPTER ONE

TONYA ARLINGTON

I never was like most children my age...always one step ahead of the bunch. I was walking by eight months old, potty trained and wearing panties by the time of my first birthday and at the tender age of five, instead of running around playing with other little girls, I spent my summers fantasizing of making it big and moving far away from East 180th Street and Tremont Avenue. As a young child, I knew that I wanted to become someone famous. First I wanted to be a lawyer, and then I changed my mind and wanted to become a police officer. I'd even thought about becoming a singer.

By the time I started school, my mind was finally made up. I was going to become an Obstetrician. I loved the idea of helping people and I loved babies, so I figured why not make a living by combining the two. I didn't want to be an ordinary Obstetrician though; I wanted to be a famous one. I wanted celebrity clients, since they had more money to spend.

I needed to make money and a lot of it, this way I could give back to my community. My dream was to build a few nice apartment complexes for the less fortunate families in the community, families that were similar to mine.

Richard and Tasha, my parents, always tried to make the best out of bad situations. They'd fallen on hard times and were struggling to raise me and my brother in our cramped, one-bedroom apartment. Even when we were struggling, my parents opened our home to whatever family needed housing.

My mom's younger twin brothers, Troy and Trey, were the last to move in. Finally after three years of hard work, saving and sacrifice, my parents found a beautiful tenant building. The apartment was located on a quiet block in the middle of Spanish Harlem. It was complete with three bedrooms, two bathrooms, a large living room and a cozy kitchen. At last, it seemed that we, the Arlington family, finally had it together. But as the saying goes, *everything that glitters ain't gold*.

When I was six, my father started saying inappropriate things to me. Like asking me, if I wanted to have sex with him. I never knew what the hell he was talking about, so I always said, "Yea," and he'd laugh. That was just the beginning of the bullshit though. Things didn't really take a turn for the worst until about a year later, after I turned seven.

One morning as I walked into my parent's bedroom without knocking, I saw my father groping himself. Instead of covering up, he continued to touch himself, staring directly at me with an odd grin on his face.

Unaware of what I'd been exposed to, I apologized and closed the door. Later that morning after my mom left for work, my father came to my room while I was getting ready for school. "Morning, babygirl. How are you feeling?" he asked, taking a seat on the bed.

"Morning, daddy. I'm feeling okay," I said, giving him a kiss on the forehead and walking back over to my dresser.

"That's good, babygirl. Listen, I want to talk to you about this morning. Daddy didn't mean for you to see that."

I turned around to face him. "It's okay, Daddy. I shouldn't have walked into your room without knocking first."

Then I saw it, that devilish grin. He put his plan in motion. "Babygirl, I want to explain what you saw. Daddy hasn't been feeling good and was only trying to make himself feel better."

I was young, gullible and curious. I needed to know why my father didn't feel well. "Daddy, what's wrong? Why don't you feel good?"

He looked away and covered his mouth from what I thought was a cough. Slowly, he turned back toward me and responded, "Because daddies sometimes don't feel good. We can't make ourselves feel better either, so we need our daughters help."

He played me like an accordion and preyed on my

innocence, knowing I'd do anything for him.

"Could you help make Daddy feel better?" he asked, opening his pants.

"Sure, Daddy," I said, walking over to him. After that, it had become part of his nightly routine to stop in my bedroom. Over time it became not me just helping him but him now helping himself to the feel of my sacred temple.

As if having one sadistic bastard manipulating me wasn't enough, one of the few people left who I trusted decided to get on the bandwagon. The night after my eighth birthday, I came back to my room after using the bathroom and found my Uncle Troy sitting on my bed.

"Uncle Troy, what are doing in my room?" I asked, sitting on my Barbie loveseat. Uncle Troy looked weird, his eyes look like they were going to pop out of his head, and his lips were chapped and outlined with what look like dry spit. Uncle Troy sat there staring at me for a few minutes with a really strange look in his eyes. It was as if he was thinking hard about something and then out of nowhere he jumped on me. I started to scream, but he covered my mouth.

"Shut up Tonya! If you scream again I'll snap your fucking neck. Do you understand me?"

I shook my head in agreement and he removed his hand. "What do you want uncle Troy?" I said as my lips quivered and tears rolled down my face.

He climbed off of me and started to pull his pants down. "Ain't no need to cry Tonya, I'm not going to hurt you. All I want for you to do is the same thing you do to

Richard."

"That's it? Then you'll leave?" I asked.

"Yes, that's all I want and I'll leave you alone after that," he said, taking a seat next to me. Seeing no harm in giving him what he wanted so that I'd have a piece of mind, I reached for his penis. He pushed my hand away and shoved my face towards his crouch.

"What are you doing Uncle Troy?" I asked, fighting to pull my head up.

"I want to try something different. I promise you'll like it," he said, continuing to push my head down.

Up close, I could see that his penis was crusty and scabby all over; I didn't want that thing anywhere near me, let alone in my mouth. "I don't want to try that Uncle Troy! You said that you only wanted me to touch it. Please stop!" I cried and tried to pull away from him.

"You don't have a choice," he grabbed both of my arms with one hand and shoved my head down on his shaft causing me to gag and throw up in his lap.

"See, that ain't so bad," he said, repeatedly pushing my head down every time I came back up. Ten long minutes later, he released my arms and pushed my face away as a stream of that white stuff shot out from the tip of his penis, just like it does from my daddy's. After cleaning himself up, he walked out of my room like nothing happened, leaving me to vomit and cry alone.

From that night on, it only got worst. Uncle Troy started coming to my room on the days my dad didn't. I'd be awakened to him shoving his dick into my face. One night, my parents left him to watch us while they went to Atlantic City for a night out. While I was asleep, Troy climbed on top on of me and started tugging at my underwear. I woke up immediately and started to kick around, trying to get this two hundred pound man off of my back. The pressure from his weight on my body made me feel as if I couldn't breathe.

"We going to try something new tonight Tonya," he whispered in my ear while pressing his right forearm into my back and pulling down my underwear with his left hand.

With all his upper body weight on my back, I couldn't move. I saw him grab the jar of Vaseline off the floor, then he took out a glob and rubbed it on his penis. With the Vaseline completely covering him, he lay flat on my back, rubbing his penis between my butt crack. "You're going to like this," he said, fidgeting around.

"Please don't do this Uncle Troy," I pleaded with him, throwing the uncle in and struggling to look back at him, hoping for some sympathy. There was none. He pushed the back of my head down, smothering my mouth into the pillow. I had no idea what was going on, all I knew is that his body was crushing me and it was beginning to hurt.

The pain I felt next was indescribable. He entered my body through my rectum. It felt as if my lower body was glass and had been shattered. I instantly began to vomit from the pain. I couldn't scream because he had my mouth in the pillow and I could barely breathe because of his heavy body pounding against my frail frame. My body went into shock. I tried to jerk my body from under him but he was just too heavy and too strong.

"Just relax Tonya, it won't hurt so bad if you calm down." I was powerless against him. I finally stopped fighting and just let him finish.

When he finally did get off me, I could no longer control my anger. I jumped up to get away from him. When I did, I felt something trickle down my leg. I looked down to see blood. "That was it Troy! I am telling my mother!" I screamed.

"Bitch, ain't nobody going to believe you!" he said, running over and snatching me up, holding me eye level against the wall. "Do you know where you going to end up if you go around telling lies like that? I tell you where…in foster care. They will snatch all of y'all and put y'all in separate homes, and in foster care a lot worse things happen then what you think. Don't believe? Go ahead and try it, see for yourself," he said, dropping me to the ground, not caring that he'd made me bleed.

I didn't want be taken away from home and separated from my brothers. "Fuck you Troy." I gathered as much spit as I could and hogged spit at him.

I've never seen a human move so fast, before I could blink my eyes; I caught a sharp two piece to the ribs. The blows sent me crumbling to the ground. "Better watch who the hell you're talking to Tonya."

That night was the first and last severe attack like that from Troy but it wasn't his last visit. It was a year later when I caught somewhat of a break. I started getting my period, so Troy stopped coming as often.

With everything I had to deal with at home, it was

hard but I managed to make it to the fourth grade, but I was struggling. There were many days when I just ran away. I never made it very far because I had nowhere to go except other family members' homes. Just to get away for those few hours, along with my time in school, was such a relief. When they did find me however, all bets were off and my ass was grass but I didn't care because I didn't want to be in that house anymore. I couldn't understand how people who were supposed to love me, could constantly hurt me and the loved ones around me couldn't see or didn't want to see what was going on.

One day during class, a social worker from Child Services came in to speak to the class. Listening to this lady gave me confirmation that the things being done to me were not normal and that there are people out there who can help and protect me.

I raised my hand.

"Yes Tonya."

"I have a friend and she told me that her dad touches her down there and that he told her it was normal."

The social worker exchanged glances with my teacher before she answered me.

"It depends on how he touches her Tonya. If it's in a way that's uncomfortable for her, then she should tell another adult or an authority figure."

"Okay, I'll tell her. Thank you."

As I listened to this woman, I began to feel lost and confused. Everything my father told me was a lie and I didn't know what to do, but I knew I that I had to put a stop to the bullshit. Later that night when my father snuck in my room, I was up waiting for him.

"Daddy, I know what you've been doing to me is wrong, and I will not let you do it anymore," I said with tears streaming down my face.

"What are you talking about Babygirl?" He moved closer.

"A lady was at my school today and she told us that nobody is supposed to touch us down there and we shouldn't touch other people down there either," I said sobbing.

"That is true. What else did she say?" he asked fishing.

"She said the only people whose suppose to touch there is my mommy or my…" I stopped mid-sentence as I recalled everything the woman said.

"Keep on, finish what else she said," he said, smirking.

"…or my daddy but it shouldn't be in a way that makes me feel uncomfortable," I explained.

"Daddy wouldn't do anything to hurt you or make you feel uncomfortable," he said, now sitting next to me. "Do I make you feel uncomfortable?"

"Yes, sometimes you make feel uncomfortable when you touch me." I was finally able to speak the truth.

"Ok well I don't want to make you feel like that anymore so I won't touch you but can you still help Daddy out."

"Yes, I can still help you Daddy. Maybe I can ask Mommy if she needs help too," I said, smiling.

My father's face turned into a scowl and his eyes squinted low. "This is our little secret Babygirl, you can't tell anybody or we'll both die. You don't want you and me to die, do you?"

I didn't know what to say, but I knew for certain that I didn't want either of us to die because of me telling. "No Daddy, of course not, this is our secret."

"Good, now come help Daddy out."

The next morning I overslept and was late getting to school. While signing the late book, my father's words began to replay and I started to cry. The school safety agent, Ms. Smith, knew something was wrong. "What's wrong sweetheart?" Ms. Smith said, rubbing my back.

"It's nothing." I tried to walk away but dropped my lunchbox.

Ms Smith picked up my lunchbox. "Sweetie, you know that you can tell me anything."

Since I started school, Ms. Smith had become something like a godmother to me. I'd always been able to talk to her about anything but this was something I wasn't sure should be talked about. Ms. Smith was persistent and after a few minutes of probing, I spilled my guts about everything. Ms. Smith assured me that everything would be ok and escorted me to class. An hour later I was called into the office. When I got there, my father was sitting there.

The principal, Mr. Lopez, asked me a series of questions. I answered them to the best of my ability. After my interrogation was done, I was asked to leave the office. Thirty minutes later, my father exited the office. I overheard him say to Mr. Lopez that he was sorry for the misunderstanding.

I got the ass whipping of a lifetime, when I got home.

I vowed to myself from that day on to never say anything about *our secret* again.

Mid-way through the school year when the things going on in my home became too much to bear, I had a severe mental breakdown. It started in history class, I hadn't been feeling well the entire day, so I asked to be excused. I went to see Mr. Lopez. As usual, he tried to cheer me up but when he went to pinch my cheek, I pictured my dad, then my uncle and attacked him. I kicked him in between the legs, broke a clock over his head and held him hostage until I was subdued by Ms. Smith. As repercussion for my actions, I was expelled. It was that day that I learned…I had no choice but to accept my circumstances as they were.

SPRING

I didn't look like your average fourteen year old female; my body was shapelier than most adult women and my features looked exotic. I stood at 5'5, weighed 115 lbs, my skin had a blended caramel complexion, my eyes were almond shaped, a small button nose and thick full lips. My breast measured 38DDD, I had no stomach, full hips, and a little ass. With my body blossoming the way it was, my father's visits became more frequent, more intense and sometimes violent. When I was about twelve, I'd started to fight back, not physically but verbally.

I grew tired of his shit, night after night…it never failed. My disobedience and backtalk only proved to make matters worse though because he then started beating my ass for random shit. If I left my laundry on the floor, I was beaten. If I didn't clean the dishes fast enough I was beaten. Sometimes he'd beat me just because and then make up something that I'd supposedly done.

September 22, a night I would never forget. Things went further than I'd ever imagined they would. I laid awake praying for a miracle but preparing for the inevitable as I heard the footsteps down the hall. "Damn," I said, turning my back towards the door but still listening. I heard him making his rounds to the other bedrooms, making sure everyone was asleep. Five minutes later I heard the floorboard by my door creak and the door open.

He was already breathing heavy, as he crept in my room. I could smell the perspiration coming from his pores; the smell made me nauseous. He bumped into my bed and then all movement stopped. I could feel that he was now standing behind me. No sooner than he stopped moving, I felt his hands prying at my inner thighs.

Thinking this was going to be the regular routine, I closed my eyes and let the tears fall silently. As I felt his body hovering over me, I cringed. I couldn't stand to look in his face so I kept my eyes closed. I laid there waiting, waiting for him to put his pudgy fingers in my treasure. His fingers never came though, instead I felt his warm slimy tongue.

I squirmed, kicked and cried for him to stop, but he wouldn't let go. For what seemed like an eternity, he feasted and manipulated my forbidden fruit. I don't know exactly how long he was down there because I blacked out and didn't wake up until morning. When I woke up, my body was sore and it burned as I peed. As I looked down and saw blood, I felt a fresh gash on my inner lip.

I started to remember what happened the night before and began to cry. I cried so much I gave myself a headache and then got sick. After I vomited, I showered and prepared for the day ahead. After my morning classes, I met up with my best friend, Alexandria Williams, whom most people called Alex for short.

"What's up, sis?" Alex greeted me as we exchanged

hugs and began walking to the chicken spot down the block.

"I don't know sis, I've been out of it all day. I had a crazy fucked-up night," I said sitting at a table that was poorly cleaned.

"That bitch-ass nigga Richard came in there fucking with you again?" Alex asked, starting to get upset.

"Did he!" I started telling her about what happened the night before.

"I don't know why you won't let me tell my father. My father will gut that nigga and think nothing of it," Alex said fuming.

"I can't let you do that. Where would that leave my brothers, my mom and me?" I questioned, sounding more as if I was trying to convince myself than her. Looking at it from my point, she understood where I was coming from.

"True…well you know I got your back, you're like my sister. All you got to do is say the word and that nigga is good as dead," she said, making a cut-throat gesture with a plastic knife.

"You're so crazy sis, but thank you for always having my back. So, what's up for the night?" I asked trying to change the subject.

"Oooh, I forgot to tell you! We got invited to the exclusive 'All White Takeover Party' tonight," she said.

"Takeover Party? What's that?" I asked, fascinated.

"What! Sis, you're kidding, right?"

The look on my face must have told her I was clueless.

"This party is only the biggest party in New York

City," she said, excitedly.

"Whose party is it?" I asked with her excitement now passing on to me.

"It's Ronnie and his crew's party. They have one every year. From what I hear, they go all out. Bottles are popped all night, they hire Brenda's for the catering and DJ Flu, DJ Ren, and Café to do the music. Girl, everybody who's anybody will be there," Alex said, making the sign for money.

"Damn, sounds like it's going to be a hot party but how am I going to get out of the house tonight?" I asked in a disappointed tone.

"Just tell your mother that you're staying at my house tonight."

"Yeah, that could work," I said with an all-new excitement about the party.

"Meet me on the corner after class. Mommy is taking us shopping."

With our plans set, we finished eating lunch and headed back to class. Alex lived a few blocks away from me in Richardson Projects. She lived with her mom, Patricia and her two older brothers, Keith Jr. and Matthew. Her parents divorced when she was a newborn. Her mom decided to split when a rumor spread that Keith, her dad, had gotten another woman pregnant. A few years after the divorce, Alex's mother decided to pursue a law degree and went back to school. Although divorced, Patricia and Keith were civil towards one another for the sake of their children. This allowed Keith to maintain a close relationship with Alex and her brothers. Alex and

I were always in the same school. We were even in the same kindergarten class. As often as we saw each other, you would think we'd been best friends forever but that wasn't always the story. By the time we were in junior high school, Alex had earned herself a pretty nasty reputation in school and on the block.

I knew of at least a dozen guys that had done something with her sexually. I, on the other hand, kept my head in the books and off the boys. I had enough shit going on at home so I had no desire to add on more problems.

Alex and I were put in the same seventh grade class—she was the class clown and I was the class nerd. One of things I enjoyed most about being in school was participating in class. I was usually the only person to answer questions in class, the teachers loved my enthusiasm but as you can imagine, other kids were not as accepting of my will to learn. One day in English class, Alex decided she wanted a shot at answering some questions. When she answered the question wrong, I raised my hand to give the correct answer. I guess this struck a nerve in her.

"This bitch think she know everything," I heard her say behind me. I turned around in my chair, sucked my teeth and rolled my eyes at her before I continued to answer. That pissed Alex off. "Bitch, I know you not rolling your mother-fucking eyes at me!" she yelled, jumping out of her seat.

"Sit your ass down bitch! You're not going to do nothing but get your ass whipped if you come over here," I taunted her. Not thinking she would actually hit me, I turned my back on her. I was used to fighting, both girls and stupid boys, so Alex didn't scare me and I didn't respect her. That's why I gave her my back to talk too. With my skills being unknown to Alex, she tried her luck. She punched me in the back of the head causing me to fall out my chair.

When I got up, I rushed her, picked her up and slammed her onto the teacher's desk. I was laying the hammers down on her ass, even bashed her head a few times onto the desk. Out of nowhere she gathered enough strength to flip me over…now it was her landing blows. She hit me with a quick combination of punches to the face and forehead. Alex was a good twenty pounds heavier than me and since I couldn't lift her off of me, I pulled a dirty move and kneed her between the legs.

The teacher finally pulled us apart and sent us to the principal's office. While waiting in the office, we found ourselves running to the mirror to look at the damage. We started bumping each other for position, which then turned into another fight. By the time principal, got to her office we'd destroyed it. We were both suspended for a week. The day we returned, Alex tried to start her bullshit again.

Instead of engaging in the drama and whipping her ass again, I decided to talk to her.

"What the hell is your problem with me Alexandria? All these years we've been around each other, we never had beef but now you on some next shit. What's up?"

"I've never liked you bitch. You always thought you were too good to hang out with the rest of us. Everybody else is running around playing, while you sitting around being a sideline observer."

So instead of asking me, what's my problem—"

"You should be asking yourself what's wrong with you," Alex said, snarling her upper lip at me.

"You don't know shit about me Alexandria and this proves it. Because if you had, you would've known that I never could or would think I was better than anyone. Instead of hating me on the low, why didn't you or anyone else ever try to befriend me? I sat on the sidelines because everyone seemed to be in a clique and I was the odd one out.

I didn't know what being a normal kid was, I was too busy fighting for my sanity at home." Alex took a seat next to me at the cafeteria table. "What do you mean fighting for your sanity?"

I don't know what allowed me to do it but I opened up to Alex about everything I'd been going through.

"Oh my God, how have you been surviving through all of that on your own?" Alex asked, on the verge of tears.

"I am barely holding on but I've been making it thus far," I said burying my head in my hands.

Having talked to Alex, made me feel like a weight had been lifted off my shoulders. After that day, Alex started spending more time around me. The more we talked, the more we discovered we had a lot in common. From then on, we became the best of friends.

CHAPTER TWO

RONDELL JACKSON

G rowing up, I was no stranger to the game. In fact, I grew up in the game. I was schooled by two of the best...my parents. Even though I was raised around the lifestyle, it was never mine nor my parent's intentions for me to become a hustler. My dad, Rondell SR., and my mom, his wife Jackie, were well known and respected throughout New York City. There wasn't a place in the city we could go and not be showered with love.

Both my parents had their own way of making money. My dad became a major dealer in 1978. He partnered with his best friend Santiago and they controlled all of the drug trafficking flow in Manhattan, from East To West and some areas of Brooklyn. My father controlled all of the Eastside of Manhattan and areas in Brooklyn, while

Santiago, controlled all of the Westside, from downtown to Washington Heights. After about five years in, my dad stopped nickel and diming. He started selling product by weight and only dealt with the small time hustlers.

My mom on the other hand was a crafty booster. Girl was so bad, she could boost your underwear without you knowing. She boosted from stores like Saks, Prada, Gucci, and Chanel for her more expensive clientele. She also hit department stores for designers like Mecca, Sean John, Fubu and Iceberg for her local hood stars. Her boosting career was most successful because she could boost almost anything—clothes, footwear, jewelry, toys and electronics. She also boosted for all sizes and sexes—adult to infants. With both of my parents making money, I never wanted or needed for anything. All they asked in return was that I excel in school.

I had one best friend...scratch that...my brother, Daryl Hilton. Though Daryl and I weren't blood brothers, no amount of blood could've made us any closer.

I met Daryl one afternoon during recess, back in the third grade,. I was engaged in heated argument with Santiago's son, Quincy, about whose father was more relevant in the game.

"Q your dad works for mines, so how is it that you think Santiago makes more money than my pops?"

"Nigga, my father runs all of Washington Heights. Do you know how many coke heads are around there? Quincy said looking around at his people like he said something important.

I couldn't help but laugh at this clown. "Man, is your

father still hustling the block? How many years has it been? My pops is pushing weight nigga! Whatever you need—coke, weed, crack, e-pills—he supplies it! Shit your pops probably still getting his work from my dad." This debate went on for twenty more minutes. It was evident who was more valuable. Quincy hated the fact that I had him looking like a fool in front of his peoples. His bitch ass pulled out a butterfly switchblade and started jabbing it at me. On a nearby basketball court Daryl saw what was going on and intervened. He ran up on Quincy and rocked him. Quincy's jaw twisted and he dropped instantly. From that day forward we became inseparable.

With a strong dedication to our newfound brotherhood, we both declared loyalty to one another until either one of our caskets dropped. Daryl and I came from two totally different family backgrounds. While I came from a structured close knit family, Daryl came from a dysfunctional home filled with different levels of abuse. It ranged from physical, mental and emotional, all the way down to substance abuse. His father was a heroin addict that beat on his mother daily because she wouldn't give him money to support his habit.

To cope with his father's abuse, his mother drank all the time to escape reality. Daryl sometimes couldn't handle the stress and often spent nights at my house. Throughout elementary and high school I soared, while Daryl struggled. After my freshman year of High School, I was skipped ahead to eleventh grade. I graduated at sixteen, and started college that summer at Borough

Community College of Manhattan.

Daryl eventually graduated but with the bullshit going on at home, he decided not to further his education. During my first semester, I configured a plan to turn my four year degree into a two year. By going non-stop, during the fall, spring and summer semesters, I earned my Bachelors in Business Management with honors at the age of eighteen. Besides my academics, I'd always been told that I was very good looking. I stood at 6'3", weighed a solid 180lbs, had a body chiseled like LL's, with a smooth chocolate complexion like Omar Epps. In school, women often referred to me as the total package. As I did what I had to in school, my parents did their thing in the streets, racking in a combined $250,000 weekly.

My father's reputation on the streets was that of a ruthless murdering man. He played no games, especially when it came to his money. Even though my dad ran his businesses with an iron fist, he was very generous to his workers. He provided all of his employees with paid vacations, full health insurance and holiday pay. But no matter how fair of a boss he was, my dad found himself on more than one occasion facing random charges because of Confidential Informants.

With each indictment thrown at him, he always managed to walk away with no jail time. Some say he had a few corrupt judges, as well as police officers, in his pocket. There was never any proof though. The Saturday after my nineteenth birthday, my dad received a heads up about a new connect named Roberto Suarez, located in Atlanta. It was said that he was offering a high quality grade of pure "White China" for a better price than Dad was paying. Since the information came from his trusted friend and partner Santiago, my dad saw no reason to believe this wasn't legit.

After two weeks of intense phone conversations, a meeting was finally scheduled. A day before the meeting, my parents touched down in Atlanta. After checking into their room, they went out for a night on the town. They had a beautiful time together. They dined at the Sun Dial restaurant followed by dancing the remainder of the night away at Magic City Nightclub. The next morning while waiting at a local diner for Roberto, my parents were ambushed by six masked gunmen. They tried to fire back, taking two of the men down but their bullets were no match for their assailants.

With the need to avenge their deaths heavy on my heart, I ignored the voice of reason and took over all of my father's territory. When I took over, I'd grown tired of watching my brother struggle, so I put him down with the crew. He started off as one of my street soldiers, pushing product and recruiting other soldiers. But after the work he put in for me on a drug deal gone bad, I quickly moved him up in the ranks. He now was my top gunner and number one marksman. Whenever I needed someone to be dealt with, I called Daryl. Daryl is as swift as they come, a master of his skills.

Most of his victims never saw him coming and the ones who did, often used their last words to describe him as a distorted shadow. Thus earning him the nickname *Shadow*. Shadow took pride in his work, a true perfectionist of his craft. His signature mark was two shots to the chest and one perfect shot to the center of the head. Because he was so good at what he did, I made him my second in command and also the head of my henchmen department.

Any up and coming Kingpin needed a infantry department. I personally believed that I had the craziest group of them all. Six personally trained killers with their own individual talents. Butch—specialized in making bodies disappear indefinitely. Golden Eye—a certified sharp shooter from the Marines. He overlooked all deals. Ghost—specialized in kidnappings. Rip—trained in deadly hand to hand combat and torture. We used him when jobs went personal. Fiyah—our arsonist. He specialized in burning shit to the ground. We often used him to send a message to a rival. Last but certainly not least, Shadow. Shadow was my gunner, he handled any job that concerned shooting, such as drive bys and things of that nature. With an assembled team like this and my natural born hunger for the streets, in no time I expanded my territory in Harlem with my new squad, The Takeover Crew. My crew's territory ran from 1st Street and 1st Ave to 125th and Fifth Ave. I, with the help of Shadow ran a crew of sixty soldiers with the numbers greatly increasing.

My father was a smart businessman and with the suggestions from my mother, he invested in many stocks and businesses. At the time of my parents untimely demise, I inherited several salons, four brownstones, three restaurants, a couple of billiards, accompanied by a few safety deposit box keys. After assessing the net worth of the businesses, I purchased five beauty supply stores with some of the stash money I found in one of the safety deposit boxes.

I came up with a concept to place a beauty supply store within every ten blocks of my territory. The beauty supply stores served as transaction spots. There was a four-step procedure for purchasing from these spots.

1. Call in you order prior to coming to the store and receive an order number.

2. When you come into the store, pick the basket with your number on it.

3. Place items equivalent to the price of your order into the basket.

4. Pay for your *items*. The cashier places all items in the bag, switching the bag with your actual order.

The salons on another other hand, had built excellent reputations of their own over the years. The Tiphani's chain of hair salons had the hottest stylist in town, top clientele and after remodeling they were all decorated with stylish décor. Each establishment was setup with four individual stations for the stylists. In the back of each salon, a lounge setting was designed as the customer's waiting area.

The lounges were decorated with two top of the line flat screen TV's, four-piece leather sectionals, large amounts of various magazines and hairstyle books and a mini bar stocked with juices, water and sodas. There were also three separate baskets aligned on the counters with assorted fruits, danishes and cookies. I hired ten of my crew members and stationed them, two in every salon for security purposes. As part of my operations, the salons were my cash drop off spots. I didn't trust the stores to hold the large amounts of money because of the local stickup kids.

The cash was picked up and dropped off every night, at different times. This setup worked because only my guards knew the hideouts existed. The entrance to every office was hidden from plain sight. With the use of a coded entry, the last mirror on the back wall slid open revealing a stairway. The stairs led to a secret three bedroom apartment in the basement, this was an idea I incorporated from my father.

PRESENT DAY

"So you ready for the party tonight Bro?" Shadow asked as we got into my new black on black, 330 CI BMW.

"Are you serious? I've been ready since last year," I joked.

"Shit me too nigga, it's going to be popping tonight!"

"Yo, before we get into party mode let's check on a few of the spots, make sure shit is legit, you feel me?" I suggested making a right on 116th.

"Yea I feel you. Let's check on these lil niggas," Shadow chimed in.

Creeping on the block undetected, I was infuriated by what I saw. There was a group of dudes playing c-low in front of the store, my lookout Jesse was distracted by this thick redbone chick and my worker Troy was not on his post at the register. With the crew still oblivious to my presence, I sped off across the street to a vacant parking lot. I grabbed my bitch Leana, a chrome M-9 from her secret compartment, pulled the brim of my hat low and started to step out. As I was leaving the car, Shadow stopped me.

"Hold up bro, are you about to let loose on them lil niggas?" he asked reaching for his piece.

"Na, it's cool. That was my first thought but instead

I'm about to teach these lil niggas a firsthand lesson in getting caught slipping."

Understanding where my thoughts were leading, Shadow just laid back and prepped himself to watch the festivities. One of the neighborhood locals named Tim saw me approaching, but I shot him a look daring him or any of the other dudes to say anything. I quickly crept up on Jesse and placed Leana to the back of his skull, cocking her in place.

JESSE

The pretty redbone shrieked and took off running in fear. *"Fuck! Nigga caught me slipping, ain't no way I am going out like a bitch though,"* I thought to myself.

"Mother fucker, you just signed your death certificate. You have no idea who you're fucking with," I yelled at the unidentified gunman.

"Shut the fuck up lil nigga, take me to safe and I just might let you live," the assailant yelled, nudging me with the nuzzle of his gun.

"Damn! what the hell would Ronnie do in a situation like this?" I thought.

That's why I looked up to my older cousin Ronnie, he had the heart of a certified gangster. Niggas wouldn't dare step to him like this. I decided I would go out like a soldier, even if that meant taking a bullet. "Nigga you might as well pull the trigger because over my dead body is the only way you getting to the safe," I said, swelling my chest.

When I felt the gun being lowered from my head, I breathed a sigh of relief. I quickly turned around and reached behind my back for my piece.

"You fucked up now nigga, hope you're prepared to meet your maker," I said, swinging my gun around. I got the shock of my life when I turned around, even dropped my gun on the ground.

"Oh shit! What the fuck, man!"

RONNIE

Admiring the courage of my little cousin, I slowly removed Leana but kept her fixed on him. If he was anything like my Uncle Tommie, his father, he'd d be trigger happy. When Jesse felt the gun being lower off his head, he quickly turned around to face his assailant. Just like I thought, he had his gun drawn but he got the shock of his life when he stood face to face with me and dropped his gun.

"Oh shit! What the fuck man! You scared the shit out of me, Ronnie. I was about to put one in your head," Jesse said, letting the air slowly back into his lungs.

"What the hell is right, like what the hell is going on in front of my place of business and put a bullet in who lil nigga…when your gun is by your foot?" I said as sternly as I could without laughing at him.

Jesse bent down and picked up his gun, never looking me in my face; he knew he'd fucked up.

"I know I fucked up big time Ronnie, I got caught slipping and I'm sorry."

"Na, you not sorry yet Jesse but you would've been had my shit gotten jacked," I said irritated. "Your ass just lost two weeks of pay. Clear the front of my store now," I said, now screaming in Jesse's face.

As I turned to walk in the store, I saw Shadow getting out of the car signaling for me to wait. We entered the store together. I looked around for Troy but didn't see him. Finally, I spotted him coming from the back room. He didn't noticed me standing there until it was too late.

"Ah, what's good boss?" Troy greeted me nervously.

I made a quick mental note, Troy's words were slurred and he was fidgeting. Cautiously watching him I continued on with the conversation. "Nothing much player, how have things been over here?"

"Everything is running smooth like a baby's ass," Troy joked. After observing him for a minute longer, I noticed that Troy's eyes were bloodshot, glossy and buldging. The longer I stared at him, I noticed he was also twitching and slightly leaning. Like a light being turned on in a dark room, it became clear exactly what his problem was. With first hand knowledge from serving many fiends a day, it was obvious that my worker had become a dope fiend. Distraught with my discovery, I decided it was time to leave. Putting on a fake smile, I headed towards the exit and said, "Tight, that's what I like to hear. I'll be back around later on."

The men exchanged their goodbyes and we went on our way. Once we got in the car, I made some phone calls and ordered extra lookouts.

"I'm putting extra eyes on the store Shadow. Troy is gone." I couldn't believe that Troy allowed himself to fall so far. I sighed and started the car.

"You know what's crazy? I've been suspect about him for a while. You want me to take care of him?" Shadow said, tapping his waistline.

That's why I loved my nigga, he was always ready to go to war for me. "Na let that nigga hang himself. As soon as he slips up, *it'll be slow singing and flower bringing for his mother.*" I laughed, quoting one of Biggie's lines.

THIS
GAME
CALLED
Life

CHAPTER THREE

THE BEGINNING

After making last minute preparations for the party, I dropped Shadow around his way and headed to the Woodbury Outlets. Already picturing what I wanted to wear, my first stop was the Armani Store. I picked a three piece, cream color suit, with matching shoes. I stopped to check myself out in a mirror. I was looking GQ sharp and feeling like a million bucks. At the register, the cashier whose nametag said Candie, was eying me like a piece of candy.

Aware of the lustful looks being thrown my way, I looked up to see if she was worth the time of day. Surprisingly, Candie was very beautiful. She looked to be about 5'2", maybe 130-140lbs…nice and thick. After a little small talk and an invitation to the party, we exchanged numbers. Next I went a few stores down to see my jeweler, Manny. I wanted to pick out a few new pieces and maybe some cufflinks for the night. As I reached for the door, I spotted two bad females walking into the Izod store. I couldn't pass up the opportunity to get acquainted with those lovely ladies.

TONYA

"Ah it feels so good to be out shopping sis," I sighed.

"Oh, you know we had to come and get decked out for tonight," Alex said, giving me a high five.

Looking through some racks, I found this bad one-piece cream color tennis dress. I tried it on and fell in love; the dress had my body like looking like *whoa*!

"Damn sis, you wearing that shit!" Alex said excitedly.

As I was admiring the dress in the mirror, I saw a reflection of a man staring at me. Creeped out, I fled into the dressing room leaving Alex standing outside.

"What the fuck is wrong with you sis?" Alex said, not understanding why she fled to the dressing room.

"Yo, please tell me why there is some weird asshole standing there, just staring at me."

Looking around for the mystery man, she spotted him standing near the register. Her age revealing itself she screamed, "Oh my God sis, that's Ronnie!"

Baffled by my friend's reaction, I ask, "Ronnie? Who's Ronnie?" Completely ignoring me, I peaked over the small door and saw Alex making her way over to him.

RONNIE

"What's up Ronnie? What you doing way out here?"

I turned to see this chick named Alex who walked up on me, catching me off guard. "Oh what's good ma. Nigga out here trying to get fresh for tonight's party."

Alex acted as if it was her first time hearing about the party. "Party? There's a party tonight, where at?"

She and I both knew she was frontin' because we popped it off at last year's party—she was my freak pick of the evening. Deciding to go along with her little charade, I handed her a flyer.

"Hmmm, looks fun," Alex said, licking her lips.

"You know I like to do it big boss style," I said, winking at her. As I was about to wrap up our conversation, the cutie I saw with Alex stepped out of the dressing room. "Damn, whose the beauty in cream?" I asked, biting my lip.

She turned around to see who I was talking about. "Oh, that's my best friend, but you don't want her. She won't do the things I do," Alex said, seductively.

Hearing what I needed, I brushed off the end of her statement. I gave *Cream* a final once-over. "Make sure you come tonight and bring your friend…uh…what's her name?"

"Tonya," Alex said, obviously irritated that I'd dismissed her like that.

"Tonya," I repeated, deciding then that I needed some of Tonya in my life. "Yea, definitely make sure you bring Tonya tonight," I said as I turned and left.

TONYA

I could tell something was wrong with Alex as she walked toward me. She had a strange look on her face like maybe her conversation with *Ronnie* didn't go well. "Hey sis, what was that about?" I asked on my way back in the dressing room to slip out the dress.

"Nothing, just confirming the party for tonight."

"Oh ok, I found my outfit. Girl, I'ma be killing them in this," I said excitedly.

I don't know why but Alex seemed to be annoyed with me. Not saying anything else to each other, we paid for our items and left the store. We made one last shopping stop in Victoria Secrets, then grabbed a bite to eat at Nathan's. Around 5:30 we headed back to the city for our hair appointments at Tiphani's, on 117th between First and Second Ave.

"You know the guy I was just talking to?"

"Yea, what about him?"

"He owns Tiphani's."

"Oh, so that's who he is. All this time we've been

going there, I never knew who owned it."

I found out a lot about this guy, in just a few hours time because Alex hadn't stopped talking about him since we left Woodbury. The salon was packed as usual, so we signed in and headed to the lounge. Three of the stylist, Towanda, Champagne and Lucy, were chatting away about the latest gossip in the neighborhood.

"Yea girl, they said that child walking around with the clap," Towanda said, shaking her head.

"That's a damn shame. Isn't she like 15 or 16?" Lucy asked.

"Honey, these fast ass little girls now-a-days ain't got no sense of respect or responsibility for their bodies. They open their legs to every nigga that spit a little game their way,." Champagne threw his little comment in extra loud, knowing Alex was walking pass.

"Fuck you, queen," Alex said, sticking up her middle finger.

"Why do you and Champagne get into it every time we come here?" I asked Alex as we took a seat on the plush sofa.

"That bitch just mad because I ousted his ass when I caught him with a nigga I was talking to."

Out of curiosity I had to know how that was even possible. "What are you talking about?"

"Last summer I was dating this dude named Terrell. We had been dating off and on for about four months and decided to go exclusive. Soon after, that bitch Champagne started acting mad funny but I paid his ass no mind, chucking up sudden weirdness to jealousy.

One afternoon, I went to drop a surprise gift off at Terrell's house. His car wasn't parked outside so I assumed he wasn't home. I figured I'd leave the gift for him and maybe even wait a little while, so I just used my key and let myself in. When I walked in, I heard female moans coming from the bedroom. I thought that was weird because his car wasn't there but maybe he had to run out real quick and was coming right back. *This nigga up in here watching porn.* I went toward his room to turn the TV off and as I reached the room, the door it was slightly open. Through the crack I saw Terrell, eating this bitch's pussy. I pushed the door open a little further to make sure my eyes weren't deceiving me, but what I saw next fucked me up.

Champagne was fucking Terrell and Terrell was eating out this random bitch. Too shock to put my anger into words, all I could say was, "Damn, I couldn't get an invite to the party?"

Terrell was so surprised to see me that he popped up, forgetting his ass was plugged up and threw his ass back too hard. Champagne screamed in agony. When he pulled out of Terrell's ass, his dick was bleeding from skin that ripped.

That did it for me. I threw up all over the carpet. I ran out the house back to the hood, telling any and everybody I could about what I saw. I haven't seen or heard from Terrell since and I heard some niggas whipped Champagne's ass. That day, Champagne was forced to come out of his fruity closet and he's hated me ever since.

"Wait, what? That's fucking crazy!" I said, laughing but not meaning to.

"That shit ain't funny bitch," Alex said, laughing too.

Three hours later we were dressed to impress and ready to get our party on.

"We are some bad bitches." Alex took final look in the mirror.

"That we are, that we are." I agreed.

Riding in the taxi through the neighborhood, I sat in silence daydreaming, imagining the day when I would leave behind the pissy projects, dope fiend and derelict filled corners, and the wanna be thugs behind me. Before I knew it we were pulling up in front of the loft.

I was amazed by the two lines wrapping around the block. I started to walk to the back of the line when Alex snatched my arm. "Where the hell was you going?" Alex asked, walking back to the front.

When we tried to walk pass the security, we were stopped by a big diesel brother named Tee. "Where are ya pretty lil ladies going?" he asked sticking out his arm to barricade us.

"Tee is it? We're on Ronnie's special guest list," Alex said in her boss tone.

"Sure you are, you and the other 200 women standing out here," Tee said, laughing at his own corny joke.

Not wanting to waste any more time with the cornball, Alex shot a text to Ronnie informing him that we'd arrived. Less than two minutes later Tee was opening the rope. "My fault ladies."

Walking in like she owned the place, Alex's aura

demanded attention.

Dudes flocked to us like they were birds and we were seeds. Some offered everything from drinks to their paychecks just to be in our presence. I was new to the party scene, so I played my part accordingly. Ten minutes into our arrival, Alex was on the dance floor sandwiched between two guys, leaving me to keep the wall company.

RONNIE

Me and my crew were up in a V.I.P. booth, having a good time. We were already popping bottles of Moet, tipping the private strippers lavishly and smoking an ounce of haze. The night was still young. Feeling my two way buzzing on my waist, I looked at the incoming message. It was from Alex, letting me know she and her friend were having trouble at the door. Shooting a chirp through my walkie talkie to security, I resolved the issue and got back to drink.

I watched as Alex walked in. I can't even front, the outfit she was wearing had everybody turning their heads to look at her, including me. But all eyes switched to Tonya as she followed Tonya's lead. Tonya's body was stacked and the dress she wore hugged her every curve just right. It wasn't long before the ladies were swarmed. Tonya didn't appear to be impressed at all by all the attention. I watched as Alex left Tonya on the wall. This was my chance to mack with her. I excused myself from the booth and made my way downstairs.

She looked so beautiful standing there, so innocent. I played my position and watched her from across the room. I was waiting for the perfect moment, wanting to stand out from the other guys who were hovering around her. It amused me every time she turned them down, she was so polite. She'd just shot down the last hopeful guy from the crowd. I made my move.

"How are you doing, beautiful? Excuse me, I meant to say Tonya." I could tell by the shocked look on her face that I'd surprised her by knowing her name.

"Ah I don't think I know you so how do you know my name?" she asked before taking a good look in my face. "Wait a minute you're that creepy guy from the store earlier, Ronnie, right?"

I started laughing so hard she must have thought I was crazy.

"Look Tonya, I wasn't trying to spook you. I saw you when you two were going in the store and thought you were a cutie so I went into the store to holla at you." I was not feeling her attitude. I was use to bad chicks falling all over me, and here this plain-Jane chick was trying to play a nigga like I was stalking her. Just when I was about to tear into her ass, the honey Candie from the Armani store stepped in between me and Tonya. I didn't know whether to be upset or glad that she interrupted me when she did.

"What's up sexy, you look surprised to see me," she whispered in my ear. She smelled like lavender and Winter Fresh gum, her scent caused my body to become alert. Trying to see where her head was at, I asked her to come back to the booth with me. While I was walking away, I turned and snuck a look at Tonya who was now the color of a beet. Up in the booth my crew was getting it popping with a few of the strippers. Shadow was getting dome from this stripper name Cocoa on the sofa when I walked in. I gave him a nod of approval.

Candie and I found a private corner, where we consumed a few drinks, smoked a few blunts, and conversed. I guess she was starting to feel a buzz from the mixture, because she let the freak loose. She got up and started tongue kissing one of the strippers named Crystal whose was finger popping another stripper named Diamond. My dick got rock hard quick, so I pulled my shit out with no shame in my game.

Crystal peeped this and walked over to me, dropped on her knees and starting polishing me off. With my head back and eyes closed, I felt Crystal's head go up and something else tighter, wetter and warmer come back down. When I opened my eyes Candie was riding my dick. I started to let shorty do her thang but stopped when I realized I didn't have on a condom. Picking her up, I started to put one on but she stopped me.

THIS GAME CALLED *Life*

CHAPTER FOUR

GOT THE GAME TWISTED

I looked at her baffled. "Na shorty, no glove no love, mama," I said, trying to put my hard dick back in my pants. Candie shushed me and took the condom. She put it in her mouth and then put it on my dick. Astonished by her talents and ready to penetrate, I turned her over. I made her spread her cheeks and went to work on that pussy.

At some point, Crystal climbed in front of Candie. Candie's face was now buried between her thighs, and Diamond was riding Crystal's face. It seemed all other activity in the room had stopped, all eyes were on me, so I put on a show. Positioning Candie's leg up over the arm of the couch, I starting beating up that pussy. She was screaming so loud, someone on the outside would've thought I was killing her.

"Ohhh shiittt! Boy damnnn," she moaned.

"Yea you like that shit don't you," I taunted her. "Umm hmmm, bet you ain't think I would beat this shit up like this huh?"

Smmaccck. The sound ricocheted off the walls as I slapped her plump ass.

"Ahhh shiittt daddy, I didn't know! I didn't know."

Feeling myself, I teased her more. "Whose got that good dick," I said, slamming into her with each word.

"Yooouu dooo! Ohhh shittt! Ahhh shittt! Go faster daddy, deeppeerr daddy! I'ma about to cum."

Obeying her wishes, I started ramming into her. I was pounding so hard into her that the couch was moving. Feeling myself about to cum, I pulled out, and snatched off the rubber prepared to let go on her ass. She quickly turned around, put my dick in her mouth and swallowed my whole load.

Exhausted I laid back on the couch. Across the room, Shadow now had Diamond bouncing on him backwards. Writing her number on my hand, Candie told me to call her later and walked out of the booth.

TONYA

The nerve of that dude to come over here, start talking to me and walk off with the next bitch like I was supposed to be impressed. After a stunt like that, this party was getting old fast. Just as I was about to signal Alex off the dance floor, this fine light skin brother walked up on me.

"Hello gorgeous, I've been watching you all night turn these clowns down one by one, and I'm hoping my outcome will be different. My name is Quincy and yours?"

"Tonya and what makes to you think you're any different from the other guys?"

Slightly chuckling, he locked eyes with me. "I know I'm different because one—you responded and two—I'm still standing here."

I had to admit this brother was smooth. "True, so what can I do for you Mr. Quincy"? I asked in a flirtatious tone.

"Well can I have a dance?"

I agreed and he whisked me away to the dance floor. We talked and danced half the night away until my feet started feeling raw, so I decided it was time to take a seat. Just as we were getting ready to leave the dance floor, the DJ entered into a round of slow jams. Changing Faces' *Stroke You Up* came on.

"Come on beautiful, one more dance," he pleaded, looking at me with those sexy eyes. How could I resist. The song was so sensual and we danced accordingly.

"Do you mind if I stroke you up…" he sang in my ear.

"I don't mind," I responded smiling.

We were really into the song and its lyrics. He caressed my ass every time the chorus came on. I dropped down and came up slow, winding my hips and rubbing my coochie against his now stiff dick. His erection definitely confirmed his appreciation. While I was grinding up on Quincy again, I spotted Ronnie watching me from the corner of my eye. I made sure to add a little more grind just for him. Quincy groaned and kissed my neck. Perfect…that pissed him off. He stormed off and I laughed to myself.

When the song was over, Quincy, being a perfect gentleman walked me over to an empty table. We exchanged phone numbers and he gave me a soft kiss on my lips. After Quincy left, I went looking for Alex. I was ready to go home. I'd had enough excitement for one night, maybe even a lifetime.

RONNIE

After Candie left, I went to the bathroom and washed myself off. I sprayed on some fresh cologne and went back to the party. I found myself looking for Tonya. When I finally saw her, she was in the middle of the dance floor grinding on some pretty boy. I think she saw me watching her and tried to make me jealous. She dipped extra low and made her ass bounce when she came back up.

I hated to admit it, but it worked and not caring to watch the rest of these festivities, I went back to my booth and got my drink on. Forty minutes later, Alex came up to the booth. After four songs of dirty dancing and one too many drinks, I had her bent over the sink, screaming my name. To be honest I don't even know why I was sexing her, Tonya was running through my mind the entire time.

I couldn't do it anymore. I pulled out, pulled up my pants and left Alex sitting on the sink cursing me out. When I got downstairs, I saw the end exchange of a kiss between pretty boy and Tonya. I was never the type to get jealous but watching them together unnerved me more than I cared to acknowledge. I don't know what came over me but when I saw her coming my way, I had to have her. I stood behind the wall next to the ladies room and waited for her.

TONYA

As I turned the corner to head for the ladies restroom, Ronnie snatched me by the arm and laid a kiss on me that shook me to the core. I was so shocked, I didn't know whether to smack him or embrace his warm luscious lips that tasted like peppermint. Not wanting to look like a thirsty bitch I decided on the smack.

"Have you lost your fucking mind. I don't know you nigga and you damn sure don't know me to be putting your crusty-ass lips on me!" I was heated.

"What are you doing with that lame ass nigga ma? He ain't me and never will be," Ronnie said, slurring his words.

"That's exactly why I want him...because he ain't

your hoe ass," I said, rolling my eyes.

"Why you fronting ma, you know you want me. I saw how you moved on playboy when you saw me looking," he said grabbing his crotch.

"Get out my way fool," I tried to push past him but he grabbed my arm and pulled me closer to him. Then he whispered in my ear, "You will be mine one day." He let me go but not before slapping me on my ass.

I couldn't believe how brave and foolish this dude was. He was seriously feeling himself. I had to check him, "Nigga I wouldn't let you touch me if we were the last two people living on this earth." I rolled my eyes and stormed away. I had to find Alex before I blew my top. I found her visibly upset in the bathroom. When I asked her what was wrong, she bumped me, mumbling something about what he wanted with her. I couldn't deal with her drunken ass right now, so I walked past her and out the building.

The whole cab ride to her house, Alex was silent. By the time we reached the front of her building, I'd had enough of the bullshit. "What the fuck is wrong with you Alex?" I asked thoroughly irritated. The look she gave me, would've killed me if looks could kill.

"It's you…you're my problem bitch!" She spit the words at me with such venom.

"What fuck did I do to you, bitch?" I was furious that she had the heart to come at me like that and confused because I didn't know what the hell was going on with my girl.

Alex turned to face me. I saw that she was crying and

I really became concerned.

"What's going on sis, talk to me." I pleaded with her.

"I'm sorry sis, it's not you, it's Ronnie. I really like him but he's interested in you," she sobbed.

I stifled a laugh that was threatening to escape my throat. "Sis I don't want him, in fact I met someone tonight." Alex's face lit up like I told her I'd won the lottery or something.

"You found someone? Who? What's his name? what does he look like?

Alex asked me twenty-one questions before we got to her apartment. All I could do was laugh and shake my head at her. "What am I going to do with your crazy ass girl," I said laughing, pulling her into a hug. Once we were settled in for the night, I told her all about Quincy Howard.

QUINCY

The only reason I went to that lame nigga's party was to flaunt my good looks, my money and bag a few bad bitches. I was at the bar with my crew, tossing a few back when these two mediocre chicks walked in. The first one was wearing this bad-ass cream outfit. She really caught my eye and her friend wasn't bad looking either but she wasn't my type. I started to make my move, but then like twenty thirsty niggas crowded around them, so I fell back. Twenty minutes later, I peeped bitch-ass Ronnie trying his luck with shorty.

I could tell by their body language, that he already had some kind of connection with shorty. I was about to chuck it up as a lost but all of a sudden, it was obvious that the conversation took a turn for the worse. I don't know what happened but it looked like Ronnie was about to swing on shorty. Just as I was sure he was about to knock her block off, he was approached by this thick honey. They walked off together, but knowing what type of player this dude was, I had to make my move now because he'd be back.

Being the G that I am, I suavely walked over to her. Instantly I saw that her facial features were as beautiful as her curvaceous body. I charmed my way in and got the digits. Now it was around 3:00 a.m. and I had this bad chick named Sandra that I met while leaving the party, bent over doggy-style in a rundown motel. If I must say so myself. tonight was a good night.

CHAPTER FIVE

WHAT GOES AROUND
COMES AROUND

RONNIE

It's been three weeks since my party and I still had Tonya on the brain. I don't know what it was, but something about her had intrigued me. Maybe it was because she was an actual challenge or the fact she wasn't flattered by my wealthy appearance. I couldn't pinpoint it but whatever it was, I needed to have her. I tried calling Alex to get the scoop on Tonya and the rude hoe kept hanging up on me.

When I called back for the fourth time, Alex stayed on the phone. "What is it Ronnie?" she answered with an attitude.

"Damn ma, it's like that between us, sheesh. I was just calling to check on you and your home girl. You know, make sure ya good," I said, trying to pry for information.

Alex was quiet for a moment before she spoke again. "We've been good, um but you should know Ronnie, Tonya has a boyfriend now and his name is Quincy."

"Quincy? When did start messing with him?" I asked.

"They met at your party. Hello??"

It was me who hung up this time. I was pissed. So that's who that pretty nigga was. I should've known. Ever since we had that altercation in elementary school, Quincy and I couldn't stand each other. Quincy hustled in the Washington Heights area, so we rarely crossed paths but there has always been an unspoken hatred between the us. I couldn't believe that he hooked up with Tonya. He probably did that shit out of spite, bitch-ass nigga.

I wasn't going to lie down and take this shit lightly; if he wanted to play with fire I would surely burn his ass. I called Shadow and told him to meet me at the spot on 110th. Ten minutes later I was sitting in his brand new, candy apple red Caddy.

"That nigga doing that snake shit son. I knew I felt eyes on me that night but I brushed that shit off and now look," I said angrily. I am not one to fight over no bitch but it was a code in the streets that real niggas followed and he violated for the last time.

"So what you want to do Boss? You know I can make

that nigga disappear with one phone call," Shadow said amped.

"Na, it's good. That nigga came in my territory with that slimy shit, so it's time to beat him at his own game. His baby mom stays over here on the east right?" I asked already plotting.

"Yea, something like that. I think she over there on 125th and 5th Ave," Shadow said, starting up the car.

When we got to her building, Niesha was standing outside with two of her homegirls. Playing it smooth, I called Niesha over to the car.

"Hi Ronnie, what are you doing on this side of town?" Niesha asked, eyeing the new platinum chain I was wearing.

"Hey ma, what's good? You looking nice today. What you and your friends got planned for the night?" I asked, setting the bait.

"We ain't doing shit but chilling on the block. Why, what's up?" she asked taking it.

Knowing I had her trifling ass right where I wanted her, I reeled her in. "How about y'all come chill with me and my brother. We going to my crib to light up a few L's and chill."

"Hold on," she said, walking back over to her friends. Five minutes later, she came back with her people and we took off to Brooklyn. I didn't waste no time. After an hour of sparking them up, I had Niesha sprawled out on my bed. She was screaming in ecstasy as I stretched her pussy walls to capacity. Unknown to many, I had camcorders secretly placed in my room. Usually they were for security purposes but today I was using them to film me breaking shorty down. Two hours later, I had successively sweated out her perm and put her to sleep. I took that opportunity to leave a special message for Quincy on the end of the tape. I let her rest for about an hour before waking her up and taking them back to her place. On my way back to the hood, I dropped the package off at one of his traps.

QUINCY

"What the fuck that nigga want?" I said into my phone. I was spending some quality time with my daughter Anniyah when I got the call from my dude Sean. I knew it had to be something serious because everyone knew not to disturb me during my father/daughter time.

"Yo, I don't know my nigga. Surveillance video showed him drop off this videotape with the word KARMA written on it. I didn't know what the hell that was all about so I called you."

What the fuck could this nigga be up too? "Ok give me an hour and I'll be over there after I drop my daughter off." I hung up the phone. Anniyah was sitting under the fan, waiting for her manicure to dry. We went to McDonald's and then I dropped her off to Niesha. As always she was sitting on the stoop with her scandalous ass friends, smoking a Black-N-Mild .

"I love you daddy," Anniyah said, giving me a kiss

before getting out the car.

"I love you too, babygirl. I'll see you on Saturday."

Niesha stood up as Anniyah ran toward her. When I didn't say a word to her, she made it her business to acknowledge me. "Hello to you too Quincy," she said, popping her gum after every word.

"What up Niesha, I'll be here Saturday to pick up Anniyah. We went shopping today, so she's straight for the summer," I said as I geared up the car to leave.

"Damn, why it gotta be like that Quincy," Niesha said, coming down the stoop.

"You made it like this, the day you fucked my brother bitch!" I said as I peeled off. I couldn't stand her nasty ass. She fucked my best friend around the time she'd gotten pregnant and didn't know which one of us fathered Anniyah. To make matters worst, she didn't bother to tell me about her the shit until Anniyah's fourth birthday. The only reason she's still alive is because a DNA test proved that I was indeed Anniyah's father.

Even after that foul shit, I still loved her but she will never know it. Being with her was a risk I wasn't willing to take but I'd lay a nigga down for her if necessary. Fifteen minutes later, I pulled up to the shack where Sean was.

"What's good player," I said, giving my dude a pound.

"Same shit, different day," Sean replied.

He handed me the tape, just like he said…on an index card taped to the videotape in bold letters KARMA was written. I popped the tape in the VCR and pressed play. The video started off with the recording of an empty bedroom. I was about to turn the shit off, thinking this nigga was just playing games until I saw him enter the room. Looking past him, the female that entered behind him is what caught my attention…it was Niesha.

For the next hour and a half, I watched him bend and twist my daughter's mother into positions I didn't even know she was capable of being put in. I watched what I thought was the finale of the tape, which was him giving her a facial shot. I was wrong, that wasn't the end. The tape kept recording as she laid there and slept. I was furious but he put the icing on the cake with the last part of the tape. This clown ass nigga reappeared, this time looking directly into the camera and started talking.

I turned up the volume. "Yo, what's up my nigga? You already know who this. If you're watching this, then that means you just seen me smash out your baby mother, a sweet piece of ass that was. I can tell by the way she wet up the sheets, you ain't been handling your job play boy. Damn she suck a mean dick too! Whewwww! Well, I said all that to say, everything is fair game when it comes to love and war. Iight my nigga, it's time to wake that ass up for round two."

I was beyond vexed now. I know I looked like a steaming bull. Nigga must have found out about me and Tonya. One thing he said was so true though, everything is fair game in love and war. He wanted to play dirty, then I was going to get my revenge tonight with his precious Tonya. I showered and dressed for my date—tonight I would be a man on a mission.

TONYA

Quincy and I have been dating for a few weeks now and things couldn't be greater. After I told my mother a few lies about the extent of our relationship, she granted us permission to *hangout*. We've been going out damn near every night since the party. My father beat my ass every night when I got home but I didn't care because I was finally living my life almost like a normal teenager. Tonight he was taking me to the movies to see *Matrix Reloaded* with Keanu Reeves. Alex said it was good. At 7:30 p.m. I was waiting outside of my building, daydreaming about what my future life would be like with Quincy.

The sound of screeching tires snapped me out of the trance. When I looked up Quincy was pacing back and fourth outside of the car. I rushed over to him.

"Hey babe, what's wrong," I asked. He walked away from me, opening the door for me to get in. He said nothing as he sped up 3rd Ave, so I tried to talk to him again. "Helloooo! Babe, what's wrong?"

Snapping out of his daze, "It's nothing babygirl, just some nigga fucking up on the strip."

The remainder of the night went smoothly, the movie was great followed by a wonderful meal at Justin's in City Island. It was 12:30 a.m. before I realized how late it was. I asked Quincy if I could stay with him overnight. Thirty minutes later we were making out, rolling on his genuine Italian leather sofa. I pulled away and tried to gather my thoughts. I was still a virgin and didn't have plans on losing my virginity like this. I've gone through the craziness at home but I've never given myself to anyone and when I do, I want it to be right and this just didn't feel right yet.

"What's wrong?" Quincy asked, trying to catch his breath.

"I'm not ready for this yet Quincy, can we just watch T.V. or something?" I asked, hoping he'd agree. The look on his face told me that wasn't going to happen.

"What the hell you mean you're not ready? We've been kicking it for almost a month now and you're not ready? I don't believe this shit."

I hadn't seen this side of Quincy before...his face looked deranged.

"I wasn't trying to lead you on, I'm sorry. Can you just take me home?"

Quincy stood up and towered over me. "Take you home, bitch are you serious?"

That was all he said before he smacked the shit out of me. He hit me so hard that I fell to the floor from the impact. I laid there crying, to scared to move. I thought he might have some remorse but the closed fisted blow that came crashing down against my temple, knocked that thought from my brain.

He beat me viciously, with repeated kicks to the mid-section, a couple more punches to the face and stomps to my spine. He whipped on me like this for about fifteen more minutes until the mirror that was on the living room wall, came crashing down. I glanced at my reflection in one of the shattered pieces of glass and the person staring back at me was one I didn't recognize. My face was battered and my eyes were damn near shut from the immediate swelling. I began to feel lightheaded, I think it was from the rapid blood lost I could feel pouring from an open gash above my eye. As I felt myself losing consciousness, he wrapped his hands around my ponytail and began to drag me. He dragged me out of the building and threw me into the trunk of his car. That was the last thing I remembered.

RONNIE

"Oh my God Ronnie, come downstairs now!" I heard Lakiesha screaming from the first floor. I raced down the stairs, guns drawn and ready for war. When I got downstairs Lakiesha was holding something in her arms, I couldn't tell what it was.

"What the fuck is going on?" I yelled. I almost lost my dinner when I realized it was a female in her arms. Bending down, I tried to see if I could recognize this woman laying there beaten to a bloody pulp.

"Where did this body come from?" I asked, assuming the woman was dead.

"This is not a body Ronnie, this girl is still breathing. I was in the kitchen when I heard tires peeling off. I came outside ready to bust a cap in somebody's ass when I found this poor baby barely breathing on the curb."

Why would someone do something like this and then

leave her on my front step? Then the feeling of nausea over came me.

"Look on her neck, does she have a chain on?"

Lakiesha moved her blood soaked, matted hair from her face and neck. "Yea, it's a name chain."

My knees began to feel weak, knowing I didn't want to know, but I needed confirmation before I assumed the worse. "What does it say?"

Using the light from her cell phone to read the chain, she looked at me with questioning eyes. "Tonya."

My knees gave way and I buckled. I didn't mean for her to get hurt. I didn't know he would react this way. Now she's laying here and barely breathing because of me. "Call 911, call them now!" I screamed, while cradling Tonya in my arms.

The ambulance was taking too long. I felt her body losing what little life she had left. I scooped her up and laid her in the backseat. I rushed over to Northern Hospital.

I must have broken over thirty traffic rules but I didn't care; I wouldn't let her die. I ran through the doors with her tucked securely in my arms. We were rushed to the ER's Trauma Unit. They were only working on her a few minutes when her life indicator flat lined. About five doctors rushed into the room, shoved me out and closed the door. They were ready to declare her deceased when she didn't respond to the first shock from the defibrillator. They were preparing to shock her again, when she suddenly popped up and tried to get off the bed.

CHAPTER SIX

KARMA IS A BITCH

TONYA

My whole body is killing me, especially from this cold metal object I'm laying on. My head feels like it's going to split in two from the severe pains shooting through it. I can hear a lot of strange voices around me. I opened my eyes but I can't see anything. *This is a bad dream*, I started to think, but whoever is pulling on my face proved otherwise. I tried to open my mouth to speak but no sounds came out, I'm not even sure if my lips moved.

These loud alarms went off. *Beepppp.*

"She's flat lining!" I heard a man yell.

"Clear!" another man's voice screamed.

Then I felt something travel through my body that made me tingle all over.. Whatever it was, it was enough to make me want to jump up and run so I wouldn't feel it again. *What is going on?* I'm trying to get off this cold thing that's making my body feel weird and someone is wrestling me back down on it. I was forced back down immediately, a mask was placed on my face and I felt myself drift off, fading to the dark lands. I faintly heard a woman voice say, "She's stable now.".

Eight days had passed when I finally woke up. My body was sore from head to toe. My face felt like it weighted as much as five bags of sugar. I touched my face and began to cry. My face was completely bandaged with thick padding. I could feel about a six inch slit for my eyes, two little holes for my nostrils, and an opening for my mouth. A strange but familiar voice was coming from what I thought was the corner of the room.

I couldn't turn my head but I could hear this masculine voice. The voice seemed to be getting closer and closer. It was difficult for me to see him even though he's now standing over me. The stranger kept saying, "He's gonna pay." Slowly picking up on the voice, I realized it was the guy, Ronnie, from the party. I tried to speak but my jaw felt like it was screwed shut.

I needed to know what the hell happened to me. I tried to speak only to be silenced by Ronnie's finger. "Shhh don't try to talk. I'm sure you have a lot of questions but it's best that you relax."

I tried to speak again and he shushed me again. I was getting angry. I mumbled "Please tell me what's going on." I used my eyes to plead with him.

"You are a stubborn lady but if you want to know the be truth, who am I not to tell you." Ronnie began to tell me all that he knew.

Hoping he could understand what I was saying, I slurred, "So you saved me? Why? When I was such a bitch to you?"

"Because you needed saving," Ronnie said, attempting to smooth my hair.

I cried all night. I couldn't believe that Quincy did this to me. Ronnie assured me that he would take care of Quincy and I promised him to focus on my recovery.

For the next few weeks, Ronnie came to visit everyday, sometimes rotating with Alex after my parents left. We became real close as he helped nurse me back to health. Everyday he would read to me, update me on the latest gossip, brush my hair and help me eat. One month of rehabilitation and I was released home to my parents.

RONNIE

During the past few weeks as Tonya recovered, I had my team hitting the streets hard looking for anything pertaining to Quincy's whereabouts. That bitch ass nigga did the smart thing and went into hiding after his horrendous attack on Tonya. I was so determined to find this dude that I put a $50,000 bounty on his head. I was willing to pay this chump change, plus more, if I could just get my hands on him. I even sent Fiyah to a few of his shops after hours and still this nigga never came out from hiding. The streets were turning up dry and I was ready to call Ghost and put that order in for him to snatch up Quincy's daughter when I got the call from Shadow that I'd been waiting for,

"Yo what's good bro! What's the word?" I said into the receiver.

"I got that pussy ass nigga's location," Shadow said excitedly.

"Oh yea? That's what I wanted to hear! So where is he and who told you this info?"

"You wouldn't believe me if I told you," Shadow said, laughing

"Who? Niesha's trifling ass?" I asked

"Na, his broad Starasia! She said the nigga been staying with her since the whole shit went down. I heard of shorty before but from what I heard, she was suppose to be his main bitch."

"Word! How credible do you think her info is?" I asked skeptically. I didn't know whether to trust this bitch or not because it could all just be a setup but then again, there was a whole lot of money up for grabs and money could make a person do some crazy shit.

"Shorty is right here! Hold on, I'ma put her on the phone," Shadow said as he passed her the phone.

"Hey Ronnie," Starasia began talking.

"What's good Star? I heard you got the word on where this nigga laying his head. What's up?"

"Yea, that nigga staying at my crib and shit."

"I thought y'all was kicking it, why would you give him up like that?"

"Ronnie, I'm tired of this nigga and his bullshit. For years, I've been holding him down and he's still doing me dirty. I'm done with it and could really care less what happens to him at this point."

"So why let him still stay with you?" I asked, interested in her reply.

"I didn't have a choice! It was either let him stay or end up in the hospital like shorty."

I was still skeptical as to what her ulterior motives where but I would hear her out. "Iight ma, I hear you so I'm going to take your word but if you fuck me over I swear on my dead parents…I will hunt you and everyone associated with you!"

"I hear you Ronnie! I swear I am telling you the truth."

"Iight Star, Shadow will let you know what you have to do."

"Ronnie!" I heard her yell out as I was hanging up.

"Yea? What's up Star?" I said a bit annoyed

"I'm gonna get my money right?"

I knew this bitch was money thirsty. I needed to get off the phone before I spazzed on her.

"Of course you're going to get your bread! Just make sure shit is tight on your end." I hung up.

I was hyped! That nigga was mine…

THREE WEEKS LATER...

QUINCY

I didn't mean for shit to get out of control like that, in fact, I'd never hit a woman before that night. When she turned me down, I lost it. I wasn't in my right frame of mind that night but what's done is done. Now I've been laying low at my girl's crib in Connecticut, just in case Tonya thought about pressing charges. About two weeks after that shit popped off, Sean informed me that the word on the street was Ronnie placed a $50,000 bounty on my head.

I had plans on seeing that man after shit died down, but tonight I was taking my lady out to dinner and a comedy show. We smoked a L, got dressed and walked out the door. It was beautiful outside, the night air was crisp and the neighborhood was quiet. Lost in the night, I was oblivious to the unmarked car parked across the street.

"Girl you know I love you right!" I said to Starasia as I opened her door.

Starasia and I have been dating one another off and on

for the past eight years. She's my high school sweetheart—she's been through the trenches with me. She stayed true even when I got Niesha pregnant. Even though I loved her deeply, I was a player and couldn't commit to just one girl and she knew this.

"I love you too daddy," she said, giving me a weak kiss on the lips. "Oh shit babe, I forgot my purse in the house. I'll be right back."

I watched her strut away. I loved the way her ass bounced with every step. I laid back and sparked another L, while I waited for her to come back.

Brrrratttttttt Braattttt!

The sounds of an AK-47 ripped the air. I felt the hot lead entering my body. I slumped forward on the steering wheel as I bled out. I was losing conscious fast. *Damn I would've never thought it would end like this...that mother fucker KARMA IS A BITCH!*

* * *

Three months home and I was wishing I'd stayed in hospital. Me almost dying didn't stop my father and his late night visits. I was so tired of his shit. I stayed out as late as possible every night. Ronnie and I became closer than ever. With Alex's permission, Ronnie and I started seeing one another and she started dating Shadow. I don't know if it was because I felt like I owed him for saving my life or because I really liked him. Either way, I was happier when I was with him and I felt safer, like I could take on the world.

One Year Later...

RONNIE

I sat in my new champagne color Lexus ES 330 with the tinted windows rolled halfway up. Shadow was sitting in the passenger seat, rolling another blunt of haze while we waited on the girls. "Yo, we got some baddd chicks!" Shadow said staring out the window.

"Tell me about it," I said, passing the blunt. "Things have been looking real good between me and Tonya kid. I'm gonna ask her to marry me on her 16th birthday."

Shadow broke his stare from the window. "You really think Tonya is the one? I mean she's smart and beautiful but wifey material? I don't know," Shadow said skeptically.

"That's the difference between you and me, I know a solider when I see one. My mom schooled me as a youngling on how to detect the real from the fake. I knew from the moment I saw Tonya she was special and now I know she's the one meant to be my wife."

Shadow burst out in laughter. "I know what all this marriage talk is about nigga! She still ain't let you hit that!"

"No, we haven't had sex yet but that's not why I want to marry her. I love her stupid," I said irritated with his continuous laughter. "Nigga stop laughing, shit ain't funny," I said, smirking.

"I'm sorry, you right" Shadow said wiping the tears from his eyes.

"Don't go running your mouth to Alex because she'll spoil it with her big mouth.

"Iight be cool, here they come." I unlocked the doors. The girls opened the doors and the smell of weed escaped the car.

"Ooo y'all was smoking that ooowweeee!" Alex said laughing.

"Shut up pothead," I joked and passed her the blunt.

"Are y'all hungry?" I asked.

"No thank you," they replied in unison.

"Iight, so we're going to my crib and chill out for a while."

TONYA

My nerves were shot! I sat silently during the whole ride, lost in my thoughts. Today marked the one year anniversary of that horrifying night with

Quincy. I would never forget the look of hatred in his eyes with every crashing blow he delivered. Whew! I still get hair-raising chills whenever I think about it.

I would've loved to have seen him again though, so that I could beat the shit out of him but I never got that chance. He was gunned down in Connecticut about a month later. When I first heard the news, I didn't know how to feel, even though he beat me damn near to death, death is something I wouldn't wish upon my worst enemy. I hated to admit it but that incident with Quincy left me scarred in more than just the physical sense; mentally I was now even more fucked up. It was bad enough that I was already dealing with two whack jobs on a constant basis at home but when I thought I had a shot at being normal, this nigga goes Sideshow Bob on me.

I'd never been with Ronnie out of the public's eye because I was afraid to be left alone. Call me crazy, paranoid or whatever, I'd rather be safe than sorry. One of the things I admired about Ronnie was his patience. He completely understood and never pressed the issue. I knew this day would come sooner than later and though I'm nervous, I can't lie…a part of me is anxious to see how this night plays out. An hour later, we were in Brooklyn, pulling up in front of a beautiful two story brownstone in Bushwick.

"Oh this is nice," Alex said as we stepped onto the sidewalk. I was taken aback by the beautiful building.

"Hey babe, are you ok? You haven't said two words since you got in the car," Ronnie said walking up behind me and wrapping his arms around my waist.

"I'm fine, just a little nervous." I figured being honest was a better way to confront my fears head on.

He turned my face towards him and spoke, "You don't ever have to be afraid when you're with me. I would never hurt you." He gently kissed me.

He took my hand and we walked in together. Once inside he gave me and Alex a tour around his beautifully decorated home. I was truly in awe with his quality of taste. His home was a two floor duplex apartment. The apartment had four bedrooms, two and a half bathrooms, a living room, separate dining area, a small office and a movie room.

The living room was furnished with all modern furniture. The floor was covered with plush, cream color, wall to wall carpeting. A 42-inch flat screen TV was complimented by a Sony surround system that sat on a beautifully crafted Ashley stand. A three-piece marble coffee table set was positioned amongst a three-piece butterscotch color sectional, accented by a matching ottoman.

The kitchen's interior was remarkable. The countertops' marble design was the same as the living room tables and all the appliances were black. An island sat in the middle of the kitchen with four stools, housing a fully stocked mini bar.

The master bedroom was the final room we entered. A king size, four poster bed, made up with silk sheets sat was positioned in the center of the room. This room had a 32in flat screen hanging low, and under it rested a wall mounted entertainment center, complete with a surround system.

The master bathroom had beautiful cream marble

tiles, a Jacuzzi, separate shower, and his and her sinks. I briefly drifted into a daze, imagining my things occupying the empty space.

When the tour was finished, we went back to the living room and had a few drinks. Ronnie turned on the TV and the last video from the late Aaliyah was playing.

"Oh that's my song, *Rock my boat*." Alex stood and started singing as if she were the songstress and we were her audience.

When she went into a slow wind, Shadow made his move. "Damn can I get a dance, you looking sexier than a mother right now girl!" Shadow said, getting up and grinding up on Alex.

Getting up, Ronnie closed the gap between me and him "Damn you smell good babe, is that the new bottle of Chanel I bought you?"

"Yup," I answered nervously, trying to smile.

"You have a beautiful smile baby, you should smile more often," he said, nestling his nose into my neck. "Would you like to come to my room for a little more privacy?" he asked, now kissing my neck.

"Surree." I moaned into his neck.

We got up and started walking toward his room. Alex looked over her shoulder at Ronnie as we were leaving. "You better be careful with my sister, negro. You hurt her and I'll hunt yo ass dooowwwn!" Alex winked at me.

As I entered the room, a feeling of anxiety came over me. Sensing my tension, Ronnie tried to persuade me to have a seat. "Come here babe, sit down with me." He began to roll another blunt of haze. When he finished admiring his work, he asked me if I wanted to smoke.

"I never smoked before" I replied. "Well let's make this your first and your last time if you want". With little persuasion, I took the blunt, lit it and took a deep pull. Immediately I started coughing and choking. I felt like I'd cough up a lung if I kept choking. "Put your arms up in the air like this" Ronnie said showing me. After two minutes, the cough finally stopped; I took the blunt back and hit it a few more times.

After a while I started feeling a weird tingle between my legs and a throb in the center of my sex. Never feeling this way before, I didn't know how to react but I did like the sensation. I felt myself starting to get moist, my first thought was to panic, thinking my body had a bad reaction. But I decided against it because I didn't want to look like I was tweaking. Instead I relaxed and enjoyed the effects of the weed and alcohol mixture.

Little did I know, Ronnie was watching me the whole time. "Are you good babe, is everything alright? How you feeling?" He looked concern.

"Yea I'm ok, just enjoying the buzz. I think I'm horny," I blurted out. My private thoughts traveled from my mind and slipped out my mouth. Ronnie chuckled because he too was surprised that I said it. He quickly went into his comforting mode, something I'd grown to know all to well.

"It's ok babe, you don't have to be ashamed in front of me. If that's how you're feeling, I'm glad you said something." With that said, Ronnie leaned forward and kissed me. I leaned back on the bed, allowing him to deepen the kiss. He started taking off my shirt, my body shuddered from the softness of his touch. He planted gentle kisses along my neckline, and down the center of my breast.

CHAPTER SEVEN

MY FIRST TIME

RONNIE

I was excited, it finally was about to go down. I dreamed about the day, that she'd allow me to make love to her and I intended to do just that. While I took a moment to let her beauty and innocence sink in, it hit me. "Are you a virgin, Tonya?"

She looked at me with teary eyes, "Yes," she said in barely a whisper.

I felt like an ass for not thinking to ask sooner, but I was already too far gone.

"Would you like me to stop?"

Shaking her head she answered, "No, I don't...but will it hurt?"

"I promise to take my time," I said, sitting up and pulling her up with me. In one swift move I unclasped her bra, revealing a beautiful pair of perky breast.

"Damn baby, these are nice," I said, taking one into my mouth.

She moaned softly, as I flicked my tongue gently back and forth against her nipple. I continued this sexual torture until her body started trembling. Thinking she was ready, I went to pull off her pants and she closed her legs. I looked up to see what was wrong and was surprised to see her crying.

"Baby, what's wrong? Are you ok? We can stop."

With tears falling freely from her eyes, she shook her head no.

"Don't worry baby, I'll take real good care of you," I said to her as I placed several kisses around her navel.

I ran my tongue up both her thighs until I reached her wetness. It was no surprise to find her already pooling juices. "This pussy looks beautiful baby, just like you," I said as I slowly took her clit into my mouth and sucked gently.

TONYA

When he put his mouth on me, I cried silently but didn't close my legs this time. I was fighting the images of my father doing the same thing Ronnie was about to do. The more I tried to push the memories out of my mind, the more I cried. Mentally battling with myself, I tried convincing myself, *this is not your father, you can relax and enjoy it.* I kept repeating this in my mind until I was able to look down and it was confirmed.

With my mind and body on one accord, I relaxed and enjoyed the feeling of his warm tongue and soft lips. He skillfully licked my treasure, lapping at it like a dog quenching its thirst. He sucked my clit with such a passion; I cried out his name in ecstasy. "Ohhh Ronnie, that feels good baby." It felt like some sort of magical technique that no other man knew, at least not the ones who'd been abusing my body.

He continued to do this mixture of slurping, blowing, nibbling and fingering my prized jewel. The most scariest but amazing thing began to happen to my body; it jerked, arched and shook uncontrollably releasing a warm sensation, flowing within my walls. My hips rocked back and forth on his face at a quick pace, my thighs locked his head in position and I shoved his face as close as I could into my folds. My body felt as if it were going through a series of tidal waves and I held on for dear life as I rode this amazing wave. I had no idea, I was experiencing my first of many orgasms. I popped up, when the last of the wave subsided.

RONNIE

I thought I'd hurt her, the way she jumped up. "What's wrong babe, did I do something that hurt you?" I asked confused.

"No not at all, that was amazing!! I'm just embarrassed by my body's reaction. I don't want you to think I'm weird," she said, looking down at the bed.

"Babygirl, come here." Cradling her in my arms, I began to explain.

"That's supposed to happen, it's normal. If you didn't react that way then I would've been worried." I could tell she was embarrassed, I continued to comfort her by rubbing her back.

"I'm sorry if I messed it up," Tonya said shaking her head.

"Don't worry about it baby." I stepped away and took off my clothes. Tonya's eyes almost bulged out of her head when she saw me naked for the first time.

TONYA

I didn't know a lot about different size dicks, but I did know his looked almost as long as a ruler and he wasn't even hard. Standing there in the nude, Ronnie was ripped. I took my time observing him, my eyes drinking him like a glass of water. From head to toe, his skin was smooth, not a scar anywhere. I stood up on wobbly legs just to get a better look at him. I walked around him in a full circle, admiring this chocolate angel that stood in front of me.

His back and chest muscles flexed when my hand grazed his body, my legs almost gave way at the sight. Stopping in front of him, my throat became dry and I was at a lost for words. Now standing at full attention was his 9in thick member. The weed had me tripping because he was so hard his dick looked like it was waving at me.

RONNIE

I smiled at her on the outside and my heart warmed inside; she was so beautiful. I truly admired this woman. I walked over to the stereo and put my slow jam CD on repeat. SWV'S *Weak* came on. Taking her by the hand, I walked her over to the bed, laid her down and positioned myself between her legs. I thought about putting on a condom but decided I didn't want a piece of plastic stopping the feeling of her perfect and pure walls. Looking into her eyes, I could tell something was wrong.

"What's up baby, we don't have to go any further if you're not ready." Even though I assured her, I was hoping like hell she wouldn't take me up on the offer because I needed her.

TONYA

"How do I ask this question without sounding crazy," I thought. I couldn't figure out the right words to say,... so, I just did it. I know I caught him off guard when I took him into my mouth. He had to bend down on the bed to keep his knees from buckling. I was enjoying myself. I It felt a lot different from being forced. I pulled out my best stuff; I sucked, spit, and jerked him until his lower body lifted up and he grabbed my head.

RONNIE

Her mouth was warm and she applied just the right amount of suction and saliva. I closed my eyes and laid back as she continued to deep throat me, inch by inch.

"Daammn Tonyaaa sshhhiiittt!"

My groaning must have turned her on because she started sucking faster. I had to stop her before our love making session was cut short.

"Damn baby, if I didn't know any better, I would've sworn you did this before," I said, half-heartily joking.

Tonya stopped and had this look in her eyes that I couldn't decipher. Despite that awkward moment, I didn't want to wait any longer; I needed to feel the inside of her. Slightly pushing her backwards, she spread her legs and I slowly inserted myself into her. She let out a cry of pain and pleasure in one exhaled breath. Looking into her eyes, I asked one final time, "Do you want me to stop?" She shook her head no so I continued.

After a few minutes of slow stroking and getting her use to the feel of my dick, I began giving her long deep strokes, hitting her g-spot slightly hard at the end of each stroke.

"Ooohhh Ronnie! Ahhh! Mmm babe, ahhh! R-o-o-n-n-nie," she cried out as I pounded into her thick frame. I could tell that she was on the verge of another orgasm because her walls started contracting around my shaft. She dug her nails into my back and screamed out as she lost control of her body.

"Ronnie, I think I'm cumming aggaaiinn! Ohhh ahhhh." She bit down on my shoulder as her release squirted out, landing on my pelvis and ran down my shaft.

TONYA

I felt like my body exploded and glued itself back together. "I know...ummm...I know," he cooed in my ear while he delivered slower strokes.

His whispers sent chills down my spine, "Yessss," I cried as an aftershock rocked me. He pulled out and told me to turnover, instantly I tensed up. The flashbacks tried to open my tears' flood gate but this time I was able to suppress them. I refused to the let that bullshit ruin this special moment.

I turned over, arched my back, and my ass spread like a map. He rubbed and placed juicy kisses all over my ass, then I felt his lips go from my ass to my clit. I jerked forward and hit my head on the headboard. Slightly chuckling, he slowly entered me from the back. I barely caught my breath from the initial entrance but I didn't have time to think. I loved every thrust. I threw my pussy back harder, matching each of his strokes as I felt another orgasm threatening to rear its beautiful head.

RONNIE

"Ooohh shit baby, this pussy is sooo good! Dammmn!" I hollered. I started feeling that familiar tingling and tightening sensation in my balls and knew I was about to cum. I was going to make these last few strokes count; I started pounding into her deep and fast. Tonya hadn't missed my stroke until then, but now she was bucking out of control. Her walls started contracting on my sensitive tip and sent me over the top; I pulled out and came all over her ass.

I lay down besides her, sucking in what little air my lungs could take; she crawled over and lay on my chest. We laid that way for what seemed like hours without saying a word to one another. I finally broke the silence, "I didn't hurt you did I?" I guess she was still in a state of shock, because she didn't respond.

I shook her gently and she drifted back to reality. "No, I'm fine." She smiled up at me and said, "Thanks for keeping your promise."

She laid back in my arms for a while before I suggested she let me put her in the Jacuzzi to soak. She countered and said, "How about we both soak together."

We'd only been soaking for about an hour, when she surprised me by wrapping her hand around my dick. I loved the feel of her hands, they felt like silk. Getting hard again, I groaned "Girl you better stop before you start something."

She looked at me and smirked with a sexy little grin. "Maybe that's what I want."

Without warning, she climbed on top of me and started to ride. It was already after ten before either of us realized how late it was getting. We got dressed and went into the living room.

When Tonya didn't see Alex, she started to break. "I know this heifer ain't leave without saying anything."

I heard the guestroom door open up, and out walked Alex and Shadow. Lost in their world, they hadn't acknowledged our presence yet. I cleared my throat. Both Shadow and Alex jumped, Tonya and I laughed.

"You ready to go girl?" Tonya asked.

Alex immediately noticed the difference in her friend. I think it was her new glow or the fact she was walking funny that gave it away. "Yea, I'm ready to go. You look like you had fun," Alex said, smirking.

All the while she was pointing to Tonya's messy hair. We all burst into laughter. I drove back to the city and dropped Alex and Shadow off first.

"Thanks for the great hospitality Ronnie. Sis, you better call me when you get in…you know I want details." Alex laughed as she walked away.

I pulled around the corner from Tonya's house about five minutes later. "I had a wonderful time tonight," I said, reaching for her hand.

"Me too, perhaps the best night of my life," she said, smiling.

I reached over and pulled her in for a kiss.

"Goodnight ma, call me in the morning and I'll take you to school.

TONYA

I sighed as I got out the car, knowing it was back to hell for me. When I got upstairs, I took another shower just to be on the safe side and prepared for dinner. During dinner, I could feel my father's eyes piercing my skin. After dinner, I ran into my room, finished my homework and crawled into my bed. Recalling all the events of the day, I smiled as I fell asleep. I couldn't have been sleep no more than three hours when I felt my bed dipping low.

When I opened my eyes, my father was sitting on the foot of my bed just staring at me. "Where the fuck were you? Being a hoe now, huh? Out there fucking and sucking right…you dirty bitch."

I was scared to death. My father had never spoken to me like that before. "Daddy, I don't know what you're talking about; I was at Alex's house."

"Do I look like I was born fucking yesterday? You think this shit is a game?

Pull your motherfucking pants down NOW!" he yelled. I thought he was going to beat me so I pulled down my pants and turned over. Instead he rammed his fingers inside of my already sore vagina. Immediately he felt the difference in my body. "You stupid bitch!" That was all he said before he started beating the shit out of me.

I laid there and took the ass whipping, too afraid to move. I cried for my mother the whole time, but she never came. I prayed that he would stop soon so I could just sleep this nightmare away.

RONNIE

After I dropped Tonya off, I went to do my nightly surveillance of my territories. Sleep is something I barely ever got anymore since I took over the throne. My dad always said, "I'll get all the rest I need when I'm dead." I never understood what he meant until I was placed in his shoes.

I turned down 115th and Lexington Ave. Everything seemed to be in its place until I noticed an unmarked, navy blue mini van parked about two blocks from my shop, on 112th and 3rd Ave. As I circled around the block to check it out, I heard the loud roar from Mack 10's being let loose. I peeled off in the direction of the gunfire as the smell of burning tires filled the air. By the time I reached the scene, all hell had broken lose.

I fired a couple of shots at a minivan as the culprit tried to make a hasty retreat. One of my bullets hit the rear passenger tire, popping it instantly and sending the van spiraling out of control into a near street lamp.

I quickly jumped out the car with my gun drawn, sprinting toward the crashed vehicle. Once close enough to the driver's side, I saw what appeared to be a lifeless or at least badly injured man slumped against the steering wheel. I opened the door to drag dude out but instead I was met by the nozzle of a pump action shotgun.

"What the fuck!" I exclaimed.

"What's good Ronnie! Surprise to see me?"

"Fuck you Sean, you don't put not no fear in my heart!"

"Ah-ha, my intentions aren't to scare you Ronnie, this shit ain't a dream, this is not pretend. I'm sure you know why I'm here. You didn't expect to just walk after taking out my man Quincy, did you?"

"Again, fuck you Sean. If you're going to pull the motherfucking trigger then do it and stop that rambling shit. Rambling is for bitches!"

Everything seemed to move in slow motion after that. As he started to pump the shotgun, my mother's face appeared. She mouthed to me, "It's not your time yet," then three loud shots rang out. I hit the ground and scurried for cover, ducking behind a truck. The fresh smell of gun powder lingered in the air. I remained on the ground, laying perfectly still. My heart felt like it was beating so hard, it felt like it was going to pop out my chest. I checked myself for wounds. Thank God, I hadn't been hit. I eased my way up off the ground and to the edge of the truck, slowly peeking to see what was going on.

Sean was stretched out in the middle of the street, on his back. I slowly approached his body, not wanting a recap of minutes ago when I approached his car. Up close the damage was clear, somebody put three large holes in him. Two in his chest and one perfect shot to the middle of his forehead. I'd been in the game for about two years now and this was my first up close and personal experience with a business related death.

While growing up, I learned a lot from my dad by observing him. One of the most important things I picked up was to never get my hands dirty. I was stuck in a combination of amazement and shock as I stood over his body.

"Ayo bro, we have to get up out of here man." The sound of Shadow's voice startled me.

"Aye man! When did you get here?" I said as we both paced back to my car.

"Who do you think put them slugs in ole boy!" Shadow said, excited about his signature craftsmanship.

"I'm glad you came when you did! But how did you know that shit was popping off on the block?"

"Jesse dropped me a line after the gunfire stopped. I thought about calling you first but figured you were already en-route home. I was shocked as shit when I got on the scene and saw this nigga with the shotgun pointed at your chest. Of course, I didn't hesitate to put a few of them hot boys in him."

Man I was glad to have real shooters on my team, the type of niggas that would shoot first and ask questions later. Perfect example, tonight's incident could have been a tragedy on my end, if it hadn't been for one of my most trigger happy hit men.

CHAPTER EIGHT

WHAT'S DONE IN THE DARK
ALWAYS COMES TO LIGHT

A FEW MONTHS LATER...

Iloved being with Ronnie. Since that beautiful night, we spent practically everyday together. Ronnie even took me around a few of his establishments, so I'd know first hand what he did on the daily basis. Since the night I lost my virginity, my father came nightly to make his inspections and just like the first night he discovered I'd been tampered with, he beat me. I didn't care though, I liked what me and Ronnie did and despite what my father did or thought, I refused to stop it. I never told Ronnie what was going on at home. He always asked where the bruises on my legs and back came from but I was too ashamed to tell him the truth because I feared that if my truth was revealed, then I would've surely lost him. One Sunday afternoon, I decided to stay home. My mom and I were sitting on the couch watching TV. Out of the blue my mother turned toward my direction and called my name.

"Tonya?"

"Yea mom," I responded, not really wanting to be bothered.

"I have been thinking on this for awhile and didn't know how to approach you, but I have to ask you because it's tearing me up not knowing."

My mother's last comment caught my attention. "What are you talking about Mom?" I was hoping she was finally ready to talk to me about what was going on, was ready to admit she knew and wanted to hear the truth about everything I'd been through.

Facing me, she asked "Has Richard ever touched you sexually?"

I just stared at her. All these years I waited for this day and now it was here and I couldn't speak. I thought back to what happened to me the last time I told someone, so I lied. "No Mommy never."

I knew she didn't believe me because she asked again. "Tonya, you don't have to be afraid to tell me the truth, has Richard every touched you baby?"

At that moment I knew this was my chance to be freed and I wasn't afraid anymore. I turned to my mother and finally spilled my truth. By the end of my horrific recaps, we were both crying hysterically.

TASHA

"I am so sorry Babygirl," I cried to my daughter. I really was sorry and so hurt to know that the man I loved had harmed my babygirl. My emotions were so conflicted that I needed my daughter for support. We cried for a while consoling each other, then I called a few family members to let them know what happened and after getting off the phone with my sister Laura, I felt this would be the best time to tell my daughter some of my hidden secrets. When I told Tonya that I had something to tell her, she had no idea it would change her life forever.

TONYA

"What do you mean Richard isn't my father? What are you talking about mom?" I couldn't believe what my mother just said. She dropped a bombshell on me.

"Tonya I'm saying just what it sounds like, Richard isn't your father. I'm sorry you had to find out like this but it's time you knew the truth," my mother said rubbing my back.

"How do you know Mom…better yet how long have

you known? I don't believe you, this can't be true Richard is the only dad I've known. How could he not be my father?"

TASHA

I knew Tonya deserved a better explanation then the one I was about to give her, but I had none so I told her the truth as I knew it to be.

"Your birth father's name is Quentrell Mitchell. When I met him I was young, inexperienced, and naive. Back then he was one of the major drug dealers in our neighborhood. He had money, cars, clothes, jewelry, whatever—you name it, he had it and I had to have him.

The first couple of months, I scouted him out. I would show up to almost all the events and parties he went to. A few times, I muscled up the courage to speak to him but he didn't acknowledge my advances. One night while your Aunt Laura was working, she overheard some girls talking about Quentrell and his crew. Laura called me and told me they were going to *The Golden Lady*.

I decided that this night would be my last attempt to win him over. Laura, me and two of our girls signed up for the night. I'd never dance on stage before, even though I always wondered what it would be like, I never had the nerve. I wanted Quentrell and nothing was going to stop me, I was pulling out the big guns. I was about to say forget it, when I heard the DJ announce Quentrell and his crew as they walked into the building.

Immediately the females starting flanking. To this day I don't know what it was but Quentrell just had this swag about him, a swag that made every woman want to be with him and made every man envy him. Quentrell made his way through the club to his VIP section, conveniently located at front stage. I knew it was then or never. The DJ called my fake stage name and I went on. I danced like my life was on the line, twirling and grinding hard against the metal pole.

There were whistles and chants coming from all directions but I wasn't focused on them. All I needed was for Quentrell to be focused on me and when I looked down in his section, there he was…staring at me. Once I knew I had his attention, I walked off the stage. A few minutes later he sent the bouncer to get me from the back. When I was finally face to face with him, I was how y'all say it, stuck on stupid and paused on dumb.

'What's your name sexy?' he spoke first 'Tasha McMillan,' I said in the sexist voice I could muster. 'It's a pleasure to meet you, Tasha.' We conversed over drinks until it was time for the club to close. I was really enjoying his company and didn't want the night to end like that. He asked if I wanted to join him at his apartment, and of course I accepted. We were joined at the hip after that night. I thought I'd finally found my prince charming.

That was until his wife showed up at my door a few months later."

"His wife?" Tonya said wide-eyed.

"Yes, his wife," I said, shaking my head remembering

that heartbreaking day. "His wife Patricia told me that, they'd been married for four years and had two children. I was destroyed, my heart shattered into a thousand pieces that day. I vowed never to speak to him again but about a month later, I began to feel really sick. I shrugged it off, blamed it on a virus going around, until I couldn't ignore it anymore.

'Bitch are you sure, you're not pregnant?' Laura said to me one night, standing there as my head was in the toilet.

'I don't think so,' I replied, dumping my head further into the toilet.

'Here, take this just to make sure.' Laura pulled a pregnancy test from her bag and handed it to me.

'Why do you have a pregnancy test in your bag?'

'Do you really need to ask?' Laura laughed. I was a nervous wreck waiting for those results. Five minutes later it was confirmed, I was pregnant. Figuring he would've told me to get rid of you, I moved to Virginia until you were three. While I was away I met Richard, we got married a year later and agreed to never mention Quentrell again."

TONYA

I couldn't believe my ears, never would I had guessed Richard wasn't my dad. But today I learned that not only did I have another father, but I had other siblings too.

"Tonya are you okay?" I heard my mother say to me. I hadn't realized that I'd been staring at her the whole time.

"Yea Mom, I'm ok…just trying to process all this. I need to get some fresh air. I'll be back later."

"Ok, take all the time you need baby."

When I got outside, I threw up. I felt sick to my stomach as I thought about all the bullshit I endured from this man I believed to be my father. My life was falling apart at the seams. I called the one person I knew I could always count on. Fifteen minutes later I walked in Alex's house, we embraced and went to her bedroom.

"What's wrong, sis? Why were you crying like that?" she asked as she closed the door.

"Richard isn't my father Alex." I began to sob.

"What? If he's not your pops then who is?"

"Some man named Quentrell." Still sniffling, I began to fill Alex in.

"That's crazy," Alex said, shaking her head. "So what are you going to do now?"

"Sis you already know! I'm going to look for him," I said, smiling for the first time that day.

"Correction, we're going to look for him," Alex said, giving me a hug.

"Sis, let me use your phone, please. I want to call Ronnie."

After I got off the phone I told Alex to get dressed. "Ronnie and Shadow are coming to pick us up and taking us shopping." I said in new spirits. An hour later, we were getting in Ronnie's new black on black Lexus

RX 300 and heading to the Palisades Mall.

"Y'all get whatever y'all lil hearts desire," Ronnie said, handing me his black card and turning us loose in the mall. We were like two little kids in a candy store, trying on any and everything we wanted. After hours of excessive shopping, we went to Oscar's Steakhouse for dinner.

RONNIE

"So what do you want to do for your birthday Tonya?" I only asked just to see what she'd say. I had special plans for her already.

"Nothing special, I just want to hang out with you guys," Tonya said shifting her food on her plate.

"That's all you want girl, shit you better than me," Alex said, laughing. "I would've been like, let me get a car, all-inclusive trip or something." We all burst out laughing. After dessert I decided it was time to take the girls home.

"Tonya and Alex, how would y'all feel about working part-time in one of the salons? It would give y'all something to do after school." I asked the girls while glancing in the rearview mirror. The girls looked at one another and agreed simultaneously.

"What made you think of that babe," Tonya asked.

"I don't know, just figured it would give y'all

something constructive to do."

That wasn't the only reason I suggested the jobs though. I wanted to keep an eye on Tonya. I had a gut wrenching feeling that she'd been lying to me about the fresh bruises that kept popping up.

"Aww that's so sweet babe," Tonya said.

Thirty minutes later, I pulled up in front of Alex and Shadow's building. "Iight see you guys later. Love you, sis," Alex said as she got out the car.

"Iight bro, shit's been real…see you on the strip," Shadow said, giving me a pound.

"Don't forget ya start work tomorrow after school," I shouted to Alex .

"Yea tomorrow at 4:00. I got you, see you tomorrow boss," Alex said, smiling.

TONYA

"I don't want to go home right now, can we go somewhere to talk? There's something I need to tell you. I just hope you're understanding when I tell you this," I said on the brink of tears.

"Say no more ma," he said, putting the car into gear. The drive to Riverdrive Park was silent, the whole time I was wondering just how I was going to tell him the truth. He pulled into the parking lot, "So what's up babe… before you even start, does this have anything to do with those bruises that you keep lying about."

Caught off guard by what he said, I just stared at him. "W-w-what? How did you know I was lying about the bruises."

"I didn't until you just said it. Yo babe, what's really going on?"

Knowing I couldn't avoid it anymore now that I was caught, I let it pour out of me like a waterfall. "Ronnie, you have to know by now that I love you, and I didn't want anything to mess with what we have. I've been lying to you and hiding a few things from you. Tonight I'm coming clean about everything and I just hope you still want to be with me afterwards. Without you, I have nothing Ronnie."

Taking a deep breath, I told him the tragic tale of my life. When I finished, I looked into Ronnie's face for the first time since I started speaking. I expected to see hatred and disgust but instead I saw hurt, pain, and something strange.

Not being able to hold it together anymore Ronnie broke down and cried. "Baby I'm so sorry for what you've been going through." He cried on my shoulder.

"You don't have to be sorry for me, just please say you'll stay with me. Please, I need you Ronnie," I sobbed.

"I'll never leave you or hurt you." He lifted my face forwards his. "Look at me, do you understand me! I'd never hurt you, I love you."

This was the first time, I'd heard him say he loved me; I started to shed tears of my own. He pulled me in for a kiss, a kiss that was so sensual it sent chills all over my body and gave me goosebumps. I was breathless, never had I felt this way before. I now knew what it felt like to be in love and to be loved back.

CHAPTER NINE

SHOW ME WHAT YOU GOT

RONNIE

I was furious, but I couldn't let it show, my baby needed me right now. The wheels started turning in my head though. I was coming up with a plan to kill Richard's bitch ass. Tonya's voice brought me out of my devious planning.

"Babe, I don't want to go home tonight. Can I stay with you? Tonya asked, rubbing on my inner thigh.

I didn't respond with words but peeled off towards my house instead. As soon as we stepped into the house, she began undressing. As I was watching her striptease, death filled my eyes instantly when I saw fresh bruises. Tonya forgetting all about the bruises, covered up when she noticed me staring at them.

"I'm going to kill him!" I screamed, startling Tonya.

Attempting to change the now tense mood in the room, she walked over to me and planted a soft kiss on my lips; my body hungrily responded. I scooped her up and carried her upstairs to my bedroom where I laid her down and walked out. I went into the bathroom, turned the water on in the Jacuzzi and returned to the room. I picked her up and carried her into the massive tub. I placed her in the warm bubbly water and climbed in behind her. I started massaging her back where the most bruising was.

She hissed out in pain. The sound alone made me flame up inside, but I controlled myself and massaged her a little softer. After washing her body completely down, I dried her off and carried her back into the room. I grabbed her favorite lotion from this set I bought her from Victoria Secret. I lotioned and massaged her whole body, leaving little kisses on her bruised areas.

Tonya let out soft moans of appreciation. I rolled her onto her back. When she looked into my eyes, a look of love and admiration sparkled in hers. I responded with a long, hard and passionate kiss. When the kiss broke, my lips were tingling. I brushed the soft stray hairs away from her face, I wanted to see every expression and hear every sound she made while I made love to her.

Opening her legs, I kept my gaze focused on her as I took her folds into my mouth; her hips arched forward and she gasped. I took my time savoring all her juices, and devouring her sweetness. Engulfed by the love and lust that shone in her eyes, I stuck my tongue deep into her pussy and sucked up all her cum as it poured from her body. As her body started to convulse, she grabbed on to my head. I slid up her body, positioning myself between her legs, never losing her gaze. I eased only the tip into her and sigh of relief came from her as we connected. Taking my time, I gave her soft yet deep strokes. I could feel her walls tug at my shaft as I maneuvered in and out of her, but still, I went as slow as ever, burying myself deeper into her with each stroke. She was screaming and shaking, having one orgasm after the other but I stayed focused. I pulled out mid-stroke. Her body jerked from the removal, then I resumed my previous tongue torture.

TONYA

I thought I'd died and went to heaven. A feeling this good had to be surreal with the way he was tongue fucking me. He picked me up off the bed and placed me on top of his dick. I happily bounced up and down in mid air with each stroke bringing me closer to my peak. I couldn't take anymore of the love making shit, it made me feel like he pitied me.

"Fuck me baby, pleaassee…baby, pleeassee." I begged and he complied.

He backed me up against the wall and started fucking

me just the way I wanted it.

"Harder baby, harder!" I screamed. He started pounding into me over and over. I was afraid I might go through the wall but I didn't care because I was about to get my shit off. "Oh shit baby, that's my spoottt… oh shiiitttt…imm abboouutt tooo ccuumm…ahh!" I screamed as my body exploded.

"Ugggghhh, me too," he groaned, slamming into me for the final strokes. His body went limp and he slid down the wall with me still on top of him. He crawled to the bed and I followed him, laying on his chest.

"I love you Tonya and I'm never going to leave you."

That was the last thing I heard because I fell asleep. When I woke up the next morning, the smell of French toast filled the air.

I almost forgot where I was until he walked in with a tray of breakfast. French toast, scrambled eggs, grits, sausages and freshly squeezed orange juice. "Good morning beautiful, I wanted you to put something in your stomach before you went to school," he said, sliding the tray over my lap and kissing my forehead. "By the way, Alex called here like a million times looking for you, cursed me out and told me to bring your black ass to school."

I smiled and dug into my food. Forty minutes later I was showered, dressed, and walking out door with him. When we pulled up in front of the school, I couldn't believe what I was seeing. I know my face had to have lost all color. Sitting parked in front of the building was Richard. Noticing the change in my demeanor, Ronnie asked me what was wrong.

"Ah, nothing babe, I just remembered that I forgot to take my pill last night. I hope I don't get pregnant," I chuckled, nervously.

Ronnie knew I was lying because my bottom lip twitched, something I hated. It only twitched when I was telling a lie it or was really nervous about something. "I thought we agreed last night not to keep anything from one another?"

I knew I couldn't lie to him. "Ok baby but before I say anything, you have to promise me that you won't do anything."

He agreed.

"Ok, you see that Accord parked in front of the school?" I said sliding down in the seat, hoping Richard wouldn't notice me.

"Yea, what about it?" I swallowed hard, barely speaking above a whisper "That's Richard, my stepfather."

"WHAT!!!" Ronnie screamed as he reached beneath his seat.

I stopped him. "Babe…you promised," I pleaded.

"That was before I knew that was that bitch made nigga," Ronnie yelled as he tried to break free from my hold. Crying I let him go, I knew I shouldn't have said anything.

RONNIE

Seeing Tonya cry hurt me deep. I sat down and talked to her. "Iight don't cry ma, I gave you my word so that faggot lives for today. Go ahead to school, I'll see you later at the shop."

"I love you, babe," Tonya said, getting out the car. "Iight ma, I love you too," I said, speeding off. I went around the block and came back around quietly. I watched Tonya put her head down and attempt to walk past that mother fucker's car.

"Bitch I know you see me fucking sitting here!" Richard shouted as he jumped out of the car and ran up on her. He was about to swing until he felt the coldness of Leana pressed to the back of his head.

"I wish you fuckin would nigga. Give me a reason to push your mother fucking wig back, permanently." I taunted him.

"Ayo lil nigga, this ain't got nothing to do with you, I'm talking with my daughter."

"That ain't your daughter faggot but if it wasn't for her I would've split your shit in two.

I am giving you a fair warning to stay the fuck away from her. If I catch you near her again, be prepared to meet your mother fucking maker!" I said, letting the sound of Leana's safety being removed add the necessary emphasis.

TONYA

I was standing there stuck, trying to figure out where Ronnie came from that quick but grateful he showed up when he did. Walking away, I snuck one last look at Richard who looked like he was going to shit on himself. I caught up with Alex during class transitions and we made plans to meet up for lunch at the diner up the block. When we got there, I wasted no time filling Alex in about what took place this morning as we ordered our burgers.

"Wait what? That nigga showed his face around here? Either he's brave or he lost his fucking mind!" Alex said shaking her head.

We got our burgers and were heading back to the building when I noticed Ronnie's car on the corner. "Hey babe what are you still doing around here?" I asked him as I walked up on the car.

"Keeping an eye out for that bitch just in case he didn't take heed to my warning," Ronnie said, tapping his seat. I loved the fact my man was ready to lay a nigga down for me; to me that was a true sign of love.

"Alright babe I'm going back in, see you in a few," I said as we walked back into the school.

It seemed like the day was dragging along but I think it was because I was so excited about my first day of work. Ironically Ronnie placed us in Tiphani's. The staff welcomed me with open arms but Alex on the other hand, had to be transferred because Champagne and her wouldn't stop arguing. I was placed on cashier and refreshment duties which I didn't mind one bit. While

I was restocking the mini fridge, I was approached by Champagne. "Hey girl, I'm glad you're here with us, we definitely needed the extra help. So how do you like it here so far?"

"Girl you know I'm happy he put me here, I wouldn't have it any other way," I said, smiling. We chatted for a while until her next client came in. "Iight girl, I gotta go make this money," Champagne said, shaking his ass. I burst out laughing "You are so crazy."

The rest of the day went by quick, I even made a few tips around the salon serving the waiting customers. At eight Ronnie pulled up, with Alex sitting in the passenger seat. I was walking out when Champagne said, "You better watch that hoe around your man."

I laughed and walked to the car. "Hey sis," Alex said getting out the car.

"Hey my ass, keep your ass out my seat," I was laughing but meant every word.

We worked everyday after school, and I loved it because it kept me away from home. Every night when it was time to close up I had the register counted, receipts typed and stored, and the mini bar restocked.

RONNIE

One day I dropped in for a surprise work evaluation. I observed Tonya mainly as she handled the register, not once picking up the calculator. I definitely was impressed;

I left and came back when it was time to close the store. I recounted the money using a calculator and it confirmed her records. While driving her home I asked, "Tonya, how would you feel about a promotion?"

"A promotion? So soon? Wow! What would I be doing, and don't say hair cause you'd lose all your customers messing with me," she joked.

"Well, you know what I do for a living besides the legit businesses right? I want you to handle the cash drop offs. You are to count all the money, have it bagged and ready to leave by the time my driver Rob comes to pick it up."

"That's it? I can do that with my eyes closed," Tonya said excitedly.

"I'm not talking about a few hundred dollars Tonya." I needed her to understand this.

"I know babe, I got you."

TONYA

The next afternoon, I was starting my new position. I was excited but nervous about the job. I questioned my ability to handle a job this important. I quickly shook the negative thoughts because there was no room for error. Midway through the day, a young lady walked into the shop and placed her bags in the empty stylist chair. Champagne started his verbal assault.

"Ah...excuse me honey, but who the hell are you and

can I help you?"

"Oh I'm so sorry, my name is Katrina. Ronnie said you guys would be expecting me. I'm the new stylist."

"Umph is that right? Well, welcome to Tiphani's," Champagne said in a sarcastic tone. He laid down the shop rules for the new girl and once everybody was on the same page, the rest of the day went smoothly. Katrina and I hit it off instantly. She was only a few years older than me and had a daughter. She told me she taken the job to support her two year old daughter and to help her mom with the bills.

As the shop was closing, Ronnie walked in. Everybody showed him love as he signaled me towards the lounge area. "Hey babe," I said giving a him a light kiss.

"What's good ma, how were things here today? I see Katrina made it in. How was her first day?"

"Everything was good today. Katrina seems nice; she can do a mean weave."

"That's what's up. I knew she'd be a good fit here. So on to more important matters, when everybody leaves tonight that's when your job will begin."

A lump began to form in my throat but I quickly swallowed it. "Ok babe, I'm ready."

Champagne was the last to leave. After exchanging our hugs and kisses, I locked the door behind him.

"Alright Ma, pay attention because I will only show you this once," Ronnie said, walking over to Lucy's station. I watched in amazement as he slid the mirror over exposing a digital keypad. He punched in a five digit code and the wall started to open. My jaw dropped and my eyes flew open. He took me by the hand and led me down the winding staircase. I was impressed when we walked the down stairs into an apartment. I think I fell deeper in love with him at that moment. He gave me a quick tour of the place and then went straight into business mode.

I was shocked when he pulled out the night's earnings from his operations. I couldn't believe how much money was being brought into the shop right under our noses. After counting out $100,000, the reality of the situation began to settle in. Those negative thoughts started to come back and just like before I ignored them because I couldn't let Ronnie down. Hours later, I was bagging all the money up while Ronnie called Rob to make the pick up. The final count was $320,000. After Rob left, we went to get something to eat at *Applebee's.*

"So do you think you can handle all of that?" Ronnie asked, referring to the job I'd just completed.

"Yea Babe, I definitely can do it."

Smiling, he gave me the rundown. Ronnie gave me a four hour time limit to have all my work done. I was confident that I wouldn't need that much time but I chose not to say anything. I would let my actions speak louder than my words. I was knocking my work out in two hours and Ronnie was thrilled.

He started having more of the money dropped off to me. I was now in charge of three salons and stores and I quickly learned with more money, came more responsibility.

CHAPTER TEN

TURNING THE TABLES

One night after coming from seeing the movie *Saw*, Ronnie gave me a box wrapped in a soft pink color paper with a hot pink bow.

"Aww babe! You didn't have get me anything," I said, tearing into the wrapping paper. When I opened it, I was surprised to see a pink, custom twenty-two special with the initials T.R. engraved in the handle. "Ronnie are you crazy? I can't carry no gun, let alone fire it!"

Ronnie laughed at me. "Ma, in this line of work you need to know how to protect yourself in case a nigga try to act up, you feel me?"

Still skeptical, I shook my head in agreement. Ronnie took my hand and assured me it would be alright. We took a trip upstate to his personal firing range. After an hour of practice, I discovered that I really enjoyed shooting. It was like a release for me. Flashes of Richard and Troy appeared on the sheet each time I fired my gun. I had to admit, it felt good putting a few slugs in them, even if it was only in my imagination.

RONNIE

I was impressed with her shooting. Never had I seen a woman shoot like that. She fired each shot with such precision. "Damn ma, you sure you ain't never fired a gun before?" I said, examining her target sheet. Almost every shot was a perfect head shot. "I'm not that good, look I missed the head at least four times." "Four missed head shots out of thirty direct hits. I bet it was me, you pictured every time you took aim," I teased her.

"Babe why would I want to shoot you? I was picturing Richard's bitch ass and my asshole Uncle Troy," she admitted.

The end of her statement threw me for a loop. "Your Uncle Troy? Why would you want him dead?"

TONYA

Oh shit! I fucked up, I never told him about Troy. Shit! Think Tonya...think. I knew I had no choice but to tell the truth, but could he handle the truth or would I lose the love of my life.

"Babe there is more than the stuff I told you before. Before you say anything, the reason I didn't tell you it all was because I was afraid that you would leave me... thinking I was too damaged," I said breaking down right before him. I didn't care at that point how weak I looked, I just needed him to understand how much he meant to me and to understand that I needed him more than my next breath.

He said nothing, he just stared at me. I could see in his eyes that he was on the brink of tears himself. This was it, I could feel it. This would be the night I would lose the only thing I had worth living for. Tears began falling from his eyes.

"Babe what is going on? I need you to be completely honest with me. Please...I'm begging you. If you love me the way you say you do, then this is it. This is the final time I will ask you to keep it one hundred with me and tell me everything because my heart can't take any more bombshells."

I knew if I wanted this man standing before me, then I would have to be completely honest with him. I wanted this relationship to last forever so I knew it was time. I opened up completely and told him everything...every single gruesome thing.

RONNIE

I couldn't believe the things she was telling me. What type of monsters would brutalize such a beautiful person. The name Troy sounded so familiar. I was racking my brain, trying to remember where I'd heard it from. Then it came to me. I just hoped for his sake it was a different person.

"Babe hold on a second, this guy Troy, where does he work?" I asked in my calmest voice.

"I don't know, I think he said something about a beauty supply store. He's high most of the time so no one believes a word he says."

"That fucking bastard is a dead man!" I yelled. I forgot for a moment that Tonya was standing there. When I looked into her eyes I saw fear. That shattered my world. With all she'd been through, the last thing I wanted was for her to fear me. "Babe I'm sorry, I didn't mean to scare you. Come here, nobody will ever hurt you again. I swear," I promised her, cradling her in my arms while she sobbed.

I convinced her to spend the night at my house. With little fight she agreed and I took her home. As soon as she fell asleep, I called Shadow.

"What's good boss?" Shadow answered on the first ring.

"What's up? Yo, our boy Troy asked us to order a dozen flowers for his mom and his wifey."

"Alright cool, should I have them delivered with his name on the cards or anonymously?"

"Anonymous. He wants it to be a surprise."

"Not a problem boss, I'll have them delivered by morning." Shadow ended the call.

Now that Troy will never be able to touch another young girl, I quietly climbed back in bed with Tonya, wrapped my arms around her warm body and drifted off to sleep.

TONYA

That Friday evening, I came in from work and my mother asked me to sit down because she needed to talk to me. "What's going on Mom?" I asked, taking a seat next to her. When I looked at my mother her eyes were filled with hatred.

"Why did you tell those lies on Richard? There was no way he could've done those things to you. I was here every night."

"Whoa, what? Are you serious right now Ma? This is a joke, right...good one lady. I thought you were for real for a moment," I said, laughing at my mother's prank.

When her face remained foul, I knew she was serious. Before I could speak again she continued, "That's my husband. What the fuck could he have wanted with you? God's going to strike you down for lying on my man. You're just an ungrateful bitch, trying to destroy what the fuck I worked so hard to maintain! You had everything plus more. What, that wasn't good enough for you? You had to have my husband too! You stupid bitch!"

I looked at my mother through tear-filled eyes. "I don't understand where all this is coming from Mommy. I told you what happened, you believed me at first and now you don't. Why? What made you change your mind?"

She sucked her teeth, took a drag on her cigarette before continuing. "Did you know that you were about to put an innocent man in prison with your bullshit. Richard told me what happened between you and him... you started. He said one morning after I left for work, your little fast ass walked into my room. We just had sex, so he wasn't dressed. He said you stood there for awhile, just staring at his naked body and when he tried to cover up *you* climbed into my bed!" She was screaming at me. "How could you? Better, why would you? Were you not happy for me? For us? You single-handily ruined this entire family. I hope you're proud of yourself."

I just stared at the woman I used to be proud to call Mother, trying to figure out how to respond. "You know what...fuck you and that sick bastard! Y'all deserve each other! Stupid bitch? I'm a stupid bitch? Then tell me this *Mother*, how does a seven year old, innocent little girl, who didn't even know what sex was or what to do with those parts of the body initiate a sex act with a grown ass man? Tell me that Mother. Did your nasty ass husband explain that too? That nigga really got you twisted!" I blacked on her. "From this day forth you're dead to me! I have no mother!"

"Oh yea bitch, you're so mother fucking grown, you think you can talk to me any ole kind of way in my fucking house? Get the fuck out! Don't ever come back here."

I had nothing else to say. She made it as clear as day as to what she wanted and who she'd chosen. I went to my room, packed all my shit and headed to the door. "I'll be back later for my stuff and after that you don't ever have to worry about me again." I refused to shed a tear in front of that bitch but now that I was out of her sight, the flood gates opened. I cried so much that my face swelled. Even though it hurt like hell, that was a chapter in my life that I was glad finally ended.

I used a payphone to call Ronnie, after telling him what went down, he told me not to worry about them anymore.

"I'll hold you down at all cost. Give me twenty minutes and I'll be there to pick you up."

"Ok, meet me at Alex's house."

I hadn't thought much about my real father since Tasha first told me about him but decided this would be the best time to start my search for him. When I got to Alex's house she could tell immediately that something was wrong. "What's up Chica? Why is your face so puffy? I know that nigga Ron—"

"My mom kicked me out," I said interrupting her rant.

"What the fuck you mean she kicked you out? Kicked you out for what?"

I starting telling Alex everything that just went down.

"That stupid bitch. I hope both of their asses burn up in a car crash," Alex said, seething mad.

"I don't know what I'm gonna do sis. I mean Ronnie

said I could move in with him but…"

"But what sis? If that man said he's going to take care of you, what's the problem?"

"I don't want to be a burden on him, Alex."

"He offered right? So how would you be a burden? You're going to be good sis, so stop stressing over nothing." Alex attempted to comfort me.

"I guess you're right, I'm going to need your help with something."

"Something like what? You know I got your back with anything you want to do."

"I want to find my father, I'm ready to meet him."

"Okay, no problem sis…just give me his name. I'll get us an address." Alex handed me a pen and paper. Just as I was finished writing, Alex's phone rang. It was Ronnie.

"Yea, she right here. She's alright, just a little emotional but she'll be ok. Alright I'm sending her out right now. Ok, bye bro."

"You'll be ok, sis. I'm going to start looking for your dad. You go home with your man and relax. I love you, mama."

"I love you too, sis."

I met Ronnie downstairs and we went back to Tasha's to pick up my things. When we got there, I saw that I didn't have to go very far because the witch was throwing my shit off the fire escape. Ronnie stopped me from charging into the building. If he would've let me go, her ass would've been mine.

RONNIE

"Yo, fuck it babe. I'll buy you a whole new wardrobe. There's no reason why you have to stand here and be humiliated. Leave them miserable motherfuckers by themselves. They'll be calling for you soon and you won't be there to answer. Speaking of calling you, we need to go grab you a cell phone tomorrow."

I saw some trifling shit in my life but her mother was going overboard. I refused to watch my woman be degraded any further so I got my baby out of there. When we got home, I got her settled in and cooked her a nice meal. Over the next few weeks things were great. I would've never guessed I'd be this comfortable. One evening we were cuddling on the couch, watching the news when a breaking story came flashing across the screen.

I turned up the volume so we could hear what the newscaster was saying. "This is Catherine Wilcox from Channel 5 News, reporting live from East Harlem on 116th and Third Avenue. Tonight, police have discovered the body of a man in a dumpster on the corner of 116th. The body has been identified from a NY driver's license as Troy Levitt, a local resident from the area. Mr. Levitt's body was severely beaten, burned and mutilated, with his penis found lodged in his throat. At this time police are asking for anyone with information to please come forward or contact the Crime Stopper's Hotline anonymously at 1-800-577-TIPS.

Turning off the TV, I turned to face Tonya. She was

staring at the television but said no words. "Are you ok?" Still nothing.

"Babe," I said, this time shaking her.

Finally she snapped out of her state of disbelief. "Did you do it Ronnie?" she asked with tears running down her face.

I was caught off guard with her question. I thought with him being gone she would be relieved but the look on her face said something totally different.

"No, I didn't babe." I was partially telling the truth.

She breathed a sigh of relief and let her emotions pour out. I couldn't tell if these were happy tears or not, so I played it safe and consoled her.

"It's okay babe, I'm here for you," I said holding her to my chest.

"It's over babe, it's finally over. Oh my God I can't believe it, it's over!" Tonya screamed out.

"It is baby and no one will ever hurt you again, not as long as I have breath in my body."

That night we fell asleep on the couch. She cried herself to sleep and I went to sleep thinking, *One down One to Go.*

CHAPTER ELEVEN

ONE SIDED LOVE

TONYA

My mother had been trying to reach me since the news aired about Troy. I sent one message back to her telling her to burn in hell while riding Satan's dick. I had no words for that bitch; she chose a man over her own flesh, so as far as I was concerned I had no mother. I should've never left my phone number for my brothers. I should've known they would give it to her, but I really love my brothers. I decided to visit them one day after my mother had left for work. My brother Taj answered the door. "What the fuck do you want?"

I looked over my shoulder because I knew he couldn't be talking to me. "Whoa, who the fuck are you talking too Taj?" I asked taking my stance ready to throw down.

"I don't have anything for you Tonya. In fact I hate you. You told all those lies on Daddy and now we don't know when he's coming home!"

"What the fuck are you talking about?" I asked, seriously confused.

"Don't act like you didn't know that the detectives came and picked Dad up the same night they found Uncle Troy."

This was the first time I was hearing the news about Richard's arrest. I had to sit on the steps because I started to feel lightheaded. "Taj, I had no idea. I wasn't speaking to Mommy, so how was I suppose to know. I only knew about Troy because of the news and even though what Richard did to me over the years was fucked up, I would've never turned him in to the police. I care for you, Percy and Sam too much to see y'all hurt like that."

Taj took a seat next to me. "You're telling the truth, you didn't know?" he asked.

"No Taj, I didn't know but do I feel bad? Hell no!" I said standing up. "None of y'all give a fuck about what that nigga did to me. It's only been about how y'all were affected! What about me? What the fuck about me? You know what, fuck this shit I'm outta here! I don't know why I came back here. I should've known that he'd sink his manipulative claws into y'all too. Y'all don't have to worry about seeing me no more…and tell you mother to lose my phone number."

Those were the final words I said to my little brother as I walked out the building. As I walked down the block I cried my final tears over the situation. I was finally free from it all. One thing was still unclear to me…how the hell did Richard get caught? I hadn't gone to the authorities and I know it wasn't Ronnie or Alex. I had questions that needed answers, so I went to the one person who I knew would have all the information I needed…Champagne.

"Hey mama, what brings you by today, on your day off?" Champagne asked as I walked into the salon.

"Hey, I just got a lot of shit going on and some unanswered questions that are really nagging at me," I said, taking a seat in his chair.

"Come on, talk to Champagne. What's on your mind?"

"Alright, I'm sure you've heard about the passing of my uncle."

"Yea, I did hear that among some other things, but I am sorry for your lost."

"Among other things, things like what?" I asked, afraid my secrets had been exposed.

"I also heard about your stepfather which is why you're here, I'm assuming?"

I wasn't surprised that Champagne already knew why I was here. "Wow you're good. I was wondering if you knew how he'd gotten caught?"

Champagne's face turned serious. "First I want to say how sorry I am about the things that bastard did to you and I hope they throw the book at his ass. Now, I'm surprised you didn't hear this already but the night Troy was found, that animal went into a church and confessed. I guess he thought his secret was safe with the pastor but what he failed to remember is that it's a pastor's duty to protect the children first above anything. So after he left, the pastor called the police and made the report. I heard the detectives have been looking for you since the arrest, to get your story."

I couldn't believe that Richard was that stupid. Did he really believe that if people found out what he was doing, his ass wouldn't go to prison? I burst out in a devious laugh that startled Champagne. I was so happy that I would finally get a little bit of payback for everything that motherfucker did to me. I had to call Ronnie and tell him the news. Before leaving, I got the detectives information and thanked Champagne for being my ears.

RONNIE

It was 8:30 p.m. and I hadn't heard from Tonya all day, since she left that morning. I was beginning to get worried. I hoped that she was ok. Then my cell lit up flashing Tonya's name across the screen."Hey babygirl, I was just thinking about you. Is everything alright?"

"Yea babe, everything is great, especially after the shit I just heard!"

I just laughed as she was telling me about that bitch ass nigga Richard. It was only going to be a matter of time before I put the hit out for that nigga. I was just waiting for the Troy shit to die down. "That's crazy babe, but you know what they say, 'God don't like ugly', now that ugly bitch will get what's been coming to him." I wanted to say something much worse but I knew how sensitive she was about him.

"That's right babe, I'm still in shock! Oh, did I tell you that I am going to testify against him in front of a grand jury?"

"Are you sure you can handle that?"

"Yea baby, I'm ready to bury that nigga under the cell."

"Well you know I'll be there with you every step of the way."

"I know babe, that's why I'm confident that I can do this. Can you pick me up at the salon?"

"No problem, give me about a half an hour."

"Ok babe I love you"

"I love you too," I said, hanging up the phone.

"Damn girl, you could've at least let me finish my phone call with wifey," I said to the back of Candie's bobbing head.

Slurrrp...Slurpp. "I'm sorry daddy but the dick was calling me."

"Is that right, well finishing talking to him," I said, pushing her head back down.

I'd been messing with Candie for the past five months. We'd lost contact after the party until I bumped into her while doing some shopping for Tonya in Woodbury. At first it started as nothing but phone conversations, then we decided to go out for dinner. It wasn't my intentions for things to go further than dinner but while I was taking her home, she started rubbing on my leg. Before I came to my senses, we were in the Crown Motor Inn fucking each other's brains out. I tried ending it there but it was something about her that I couldn't leave alone.

TONYA

Over the next three weeks, I prepared myself mentally to take the stand against Richard. I hadn't seen him since the incident in front of my school almost a year ago. Today was the first day of my new beginning. I was nervous about taking the stand, but the feeling soon passed when I thought about the gratification I would get behind his sentencing. When I walked into the waiting area, I saw Tasha sitting there with my Aunt Barbara.

Attempting to walk pass them failed when Tasha grabbed my hand. "Babygirl, I'm sorry it had to come to this. Richard told me the whole truth and I am sorry I took his side over yours. Can you ever forgive me?"

"Why the sudden change of heart? What do you want from me? No matter what you say, I'm going in there and telling it all. You worried about him? You better pray that they don't come out here and arrest your ass too."

"Listen Tonya, I know you're going to do what you have to do but I think you should read these letters from Richard."

She handed me a bag full of letters addressed to me from Richard while he'd been incarcerated. Figuring I had some time until they called me in, I took the bag from her. I sat in the corner of the waiting area and read letter after letter. By the time I was called my head was messed up. The things he wrote about while being in prison broke my heart into thousands of little pieces. Looking up from the last letter, I saw him; he was handcuffed and being escorted by two police officers. Our eyes locked and for a brief second I thought I saw a tear fall from his left eye. I started to feel bad but then the inner abused child came out and smacked the common sense back into place. I sat before the grand jury and answered every question directed at me. After my testimony, I was informed that the grand jury would be back with a decision in a few hours.

When I walked out of the courtroom Tasha came rushing towards me. I thought she was going to attack me so I braced myself, prepared to fight her if I had to. As she got closer, I could see that she'd been crying.

"Tonya, words can't express how sorry I am, sitting there listening to you speak with such details just made it clear to me that you were telling the truth. I don't know how I'll make things between us right but I will do it somehow."

She reached out her arms to give me a hug but I resisted.

"It's okay, I'm determined to fix this, you'll see," she said as she walked away and took a seat in the corridor.

I didn't know about her but I was staying, I would see

this through to the end. Two hours later, the grand jury returned with their decision. Richard was charged with multiple counts of child molestation, endangerment of a child and child abuse. Once their decision was revealed, I heard the loud wails from Tasha, echoing throughout the courtroom. I shed some tears too but my tears were of joy…finally he would pay.

Throughout the day I looked around for Ronnie but he never showed up. I couldn't understand why he wasn't there but I sure hoped it was for a good reason.

RONNIE

"Uughh damn ma, this shit is wet! I said thrusting into Candie's thick frame.

"Ummm daddy, this dick feels soooo good."

This girl's pussy never ceased to amaze me, it was always wet and tight. Her back walls had a vise like grip around the tip of my dick and her sensitive canal was sucking the rest of me in like a vacuum. I loved Tonya dearly but there were just some things I couldn't teach her sexually and Candie seemed to have her PHD in sexology.

She threw her ass back like a pro. I loved to see the waves of ass coming back at me. I sped up my stroke as I felt my nut building in the base of my balls. My balls had become a bit sensitive from slapping against her swollen lips. She reached under and caressed them. Damn she knew how to bring a nigga into a blissful heaven. "Dammmn!" was the only word that came from me as I let my seed spill into her womanly garden, something I'd become comfortable with.

"Damn that was on point as usual," I said, grabbing the rag out of the bowl of water sitting on the dresser. The rag sent a shock through my body when I put the cool rag on my sensitive tip. I rolled over to the other nightstand and opened the flip to my razor phone. I had twenty missed calls, ten new voice mails, and five text messages—all from Tonya.

I played the voicemails first. An angry Tonya streamed through. "What the fuck happened to you today Ronnie? You told me that you would be there for me. On one of the most important days of my life, you were a no-call no-show. You know how traumatic this whole ordeal has been for me and you didn't even have the decency to call me and let me know everything was alright. I hope whatever you were doing was worth it. I'm going to my mom's tonight. Maybe I'll be home tomorrow; I can't stand to see you right now."

That was the first message of the ten, so I already had a pretty good idea what the others said. "Fuck!" I shouted. *How the hell did I forget she was facing the grand jury today?*

"What's wrong babe?" Candie said, rubbing my shoulders.

"I forgot about Tonya's court appearance today and she's livid right now," I said, lying back in her lap.

"Oh shit, so you better getting going; I understand you got to take care of home."

Shit like that was why I couldn't leave her, she was a real down ass chick. "Na its good ma, she said she ain't going home tonight so since she won't be there, there's no reason to go home to an empty house. I climbed over her, laid on my back and pulled her on top of me.

"You ain't done yet"

"Ok, this time I'm putting you to sleep," she said as she began to ride me into a deep slumber.

TONYA

It's been a month and I still hadn't spoken to Ronnie. I didn't return his calls, I refused his flower deliveries at the shop, and I made Alex promise she wouldn't relay any messages from him to me. I had nothing for him. Him not being there for me when I needed him the most, did things to my heart. A good thing came out of my heartache though, my mother and I were kind of on speaking terms now and my brothers started coming around too. I continued to work everyday and didn't stay a minute longer than I had to.

Katrina and I started spending a lot of time together after work. Alex wasn't available most of the time, now that her and Shadow had become really serious. That was ok with me because Katrina was cool to be around. She took me to meet her daughter. I had a great time with them; they seemed like a happy family. I often reflected what it would be like to have that feeling again.

CHAPTER TWELVE

ALL GOOD THINGS
COME TO AN END

On the night of my sixteenth birthday, I was sitting at home eating away my sorrows when my phone rang. It was Alex.

"Hey bitch, what you doing?"

"Hey bitch, I'm not doing shit but watching TV and eating icecream"

"What the fuck bitch, it's your motherfucking birthday! Ayo get your ass up and look in the bottom of your closet"

I wonder what this girl could be up to now, I thought to myself as I walked to the closet.

"Ain't shit in here Alex but my dirty laundry bags."

Alex started laughing. "Pick up the bags dummy."

When I lifted the bags, a long wrapped box laid under them.

"Aww, thanks sis" I said with excitement building up.

"Ah shut up with that mushy shit and open the box." Opening the box, I laid my eyes on this sexy red dress with matching shoes and clutch bag.

I took the dress out the box and held it to my skin.

"Sis, you didn't have to do this," I said, getting chocked up with emotion.

"Open your door so I can see how you look."

"Open my door?"

"Yea, open the door hussy."

Unlocking the front door, I saw Alex standing there in a beautiful, royal blue dress with her makeup bag in her hand.

"Why you all are dressed up sis?"

"You really didn't think I was going to let you sit in the house on your birthday, did you? Now go shower and hurry up so I can do something with your hair."

That's why I loved that girl, she knew how to cheer me up no matter how deep in a rut I was in.

"Where are we going?"

"To my cousin's birthday bash at *Scream,* that teenage club in the Bronx."

"Oh, ok." I hurried to the bathroom to shower. Thirty minutes later I was dressed, makeup done and Alex did her rendition of Whitney's New Year hair style from *Waiting to Exhale* on me.

When we arrived at the club, we were escorted to the lower level. As we reached the section where her cousin's setup was supposed to be, a pair of hands quickly covered my eyes. When the mystery person moved their hands, I was greeted with a loud "SURPRISE!" All my closest friends and family were standing in front of me. The mystery person stepped from behind me and I stood face to face with my love, Ronnie.

"Oh my God Ronnie, did you do all this for me?" I cried happy tears, not caring that I was probably messing up my makeup.

"Yes I did, with the help of Alex and your mother."

Just then my mom stepped out of a corner. I ran over to her and gave her the biggest hug, then Alex. "I can't believe y'all did all of this for me, especially you Ronnie after the way I've been acting. I love you so much." I walked into his warm embracing arms.

"It's alright ma, I fucked up big time and I paid the price but that was no reason to let it stop this party. I've been planning it since your fifteenth birthday," Ronnie said, laughing.

DJ Clue started his spin and we partied hard. Everyone was there, even Katrina and Champagne. We had a blast, this was the best night of my life.

RONNIE

Around 11:30 I had the lights dimmed and the DJ killed the music. I asked Tonya to come to the center of the dance floor. I placed a chair there for her and grabbed

Marie A. Norfleet

the microphone. Once it was completely quiet and all eyes were on us, I dropped on one knee. "Tonya, this last year and half has been the greatest of my life. Never would I have imagined that the day I laid eyes on you in the Izod Store, would be the day I laid eyes on my better half...my soul mate. With you I've been able to be open and honest about any and everything and never had to worry about you judging me. Today, before all your family and friends, I'm asking you to be my wife. Will you marry me, Tonya?"

I pulled out the 2.0 carat diamond, white gold engagement ring I purchased a several months back. Tonya's body started to shake and she began crying.

"Tonya are you ok? Babygirl talk to me."

"Yes!! Oh my God!! Yes, of course I'll marry you Ronnie!" Tonya screamed and jumped on me. She caught me so off guard that I lost my balance and we hit the floor. The crowd erupted in laughter, applause and chants of congratulations.

In the midst of the celebration a woman rushed from the crowd toward the dance floor. "Hold the fuck up Rondell! Now I've been content with being your side bitch for a while now, but I'll be damned if you think you're going to marry this bitch. You must have lost your fucking mind. I've been the one cradling your ass through the night when you had those anxiety attacks. It's my ear that you complain into about her. It's me cooking breakfast for you on the mornings you told her you were grinding. It's also me that's going to bear your first child and you're talking about you're going to marry her—fuck outta here! That shit just ain't going down!"

My jaw dropped to the ground and my heart sped up about forty beats when Candie finished her little speech.

"Is what she saying true Ronnie?"

I was so shocked, I forgot Tonya was there and had just heard everything.

"Ronnie, please tell me she's lying. Please Ronnie, tell me you haven't done those things she just said." Tonya was now hysterical.

I told myself from the day I became involved with her that I would never lie to her about anything so I came clean. "Yes, yes, everything she said is true except the fact that she's not pregnant and I never complained about you. I love you." I spoke with confidence.

"No that's where you're wrong Ronnie," Candie said, walking towards me with a zip lock bag in one hand and some sort of picture in the other.

The zip lock bag contained three different pregnancy test, all positive. The picture she held in her hand was a sonogram of a three month old embryo.

TONYA

I don't know what came over me but watching those two standing there together set off something in me. I swiftly walked over to the chair I had been sitting in, picked it up and bashed Ronnie in the back of his head. He dropped to the floor.

"You swore you would never hurt me!" I screamed, kicking him in his back while trying to steady myself in my heels. The last kick I gave him twisted my foot and I collapsed on top of him. "Why Ronnie? Why would you do this to us? I thought you loved me?" I cried, lying on his semi-conscious body.

I heard commotion coming from near the DJ booth. When I looked over, I saw Alex going to work on the woman who just shattered my world. I got up and rushed over to stop Alex from killing her.

"Alex stop! Stop Alex, she's pregnant! She's pregnant!" I yelled at Alex as I tried to pull her off. Finally I managed to fling Alex away from her.

"Move Tonya, that bitch thought she was big and bad walking in here with that bullshit. Move Tonya…move!" Alex screamed but I wouldn't let her go. She would not being going to jail for killing this woman's unborn child. "I'm going to see you again bitch, I promise you that!" Alex spat over my shoulder as I dragged her out the club.

I cried the whole ride to Alex's house, my world as I knew it was over. We walked slowly into Alex's house, heels in hands, me crying and Alex holding me tight.

Once inside, I collapsed on her couch. "How could I have been so naive Alex? I never thought he'd do me dirty like that?"

"Some niggas ain't shit, sis and I am sorry the wrong ones keep coming into your life." Alex rocked me in her arms until I feel asleep. I tossed and turned throughout the night, as the scene at my party replayed over and over again. About 3:30 a.m. I crept out of Alex's house. I just wanted to be alone.

RONNIE

By the time I came to, Tonya was long gone. I couldn't believe she hit me with a damn chair. I started to give the word to Shadow but calmed myself down. This whole shit was my fault anyway. I don't know why I hadn't stopped fucking with Candie when I had the chance. I found Candie surrounded by EMS workers and police.

"What happened Candie? Are you alright?"

"Hell no, I'm not alright. Your lil girlfriend's buddy attacked me. I'm pressing charges on that bitch and then I'm going to the hospital to check on *our* baby!"

I'd forgotten all about the baby. "Excuse me officers, may I speak with her alone for a moment!"

"Make it quick," the officer snapped.

After they were out of hearing distance I tore into her ass. "What the fuck were you thinking, showing up here and making a fucking scene. The pregnancy news is something we should've discussed privately. Why did you feel the need to broadcast it here…especially tonight? Secondly how the hell did you even know I was here?"

"First off, don't talk to me like I'm some lame bitch. I overhead you the other night on the phone talking to Shadow about your plans for tonight. I found the ring a couple of weeks ago but didn't think you had plans on using it anytime soon. When I heard you on the phone, I had to stop you.

"So why didn't you say something beforehand? Why wait until tonight? And how long have you known you were pregnant?"

"I started having my suspicions about the pregnancy two weeks ago when I realized that my period hadn't come yet. I took the home pregnancy tests and they were positive so I called and scheduled an appointment. At my appointment yesterday it was confirmed. I tried to call you yesterday so that we could've had lunch and discussed it but you forwarded all my calls to voicemail, so I knew I had to come here. I didn't intend on blowing up like that but when I walked in and saw you proposing to her, something snapped. I'm sorry for the way I went about it, but you needed to know the truth."

I took a seat next to her. "Ok listen, don't press charges on Alex. She was acting in her friend's defense. I'll take you to the hospital and we can talk about what we're going to do."

It was 4:00 in the morning and I'd just dropped Candie off when I got the call from Alex.

"What is it Alex, I really don't feel like talking about last night!"

"I ain't calling for that right now, Ronnie. I was calling to see if you'd seen Tonya?"

"I haven't seen Tonya since she knocked me out with that damn chair, I thought she left with you."

"She did but when I woke up fifteen minutes ago she was gone! I tried calling her cell, but it went straight to voicemail. I was hoping she'd gone to your house maybe to talk or something."

"Well I haven't seen or heard from her. Did you check her mom's place?"

"No, not yet. My first thought was to call you but I'm going to take a walk over there now. Should I call you if I find her?"

"Yea, be sure to do that." I hung up the phone.

TONYA

After I left Alex's house, I walked around the neighborhood for a while. I just walked and thought until I got tired. I sat down in my mother's hallway and before I knew it I fell. I was awakened by someone nudging me. When I opened my eyes, Alex was standing over me.

"Why did you leave, sis? I've been looking all over for you."

"I couldn't sleep so I went for a walk, Mom," I said, teasing her.

"Say what you want but I was worried about you. Why weren't you answering your phone at least?"

I pulled out my phone. "The battery was dead, that's why," I said, showing her the phone.

"Well, I'm glad you're alright. I got something for you. I was going to give it to you last night but all that drama popped off."

Alex pulled out an envelope and passed it to me. As

soon as I saw the contents inside, I began to cry. Inside there was a card with the title *New Beginnings*. Inside the card was an address for my biological father.

"Thank you, thank you, thank you!" I screamed, hugging Alex so hard I damn near squeezed the life out of her.

"Well damn, can I live?" Alex said, playfully pushing me away.

"This is just…WOW! I can't believe this is real. Is this legit Alex?"

"Legit? Did you really just ask me that?"

I could tell that I'd offended her. "I'm sorry sis, I didn't mean it like that. I'm just so happy right now! How did you find this info?"

The smile returned to her face. "The internet is an amazing thing and that's all I'm saying. Now go upstairs and get changed so we can embark on this new journey.

I was still in a state of disbelief when I came back down. "Pinch me and tell me it ain't a dream," I said.

Alex must've called Shadow because when we stepped out the door he was parked out front waiting for us. When we got in, I could sense a little tension but I said hello, never mentioned last night or Ronnie. Three hours later, we pulled across the street from the address Alex had found to a house in Helderburg, Albany. I was in awe as I gawked at the outer beauty of his home. A lighted stone pathway led to the beautiful bold door, bricks the color of sand made-up the structure of the house, a swing hung from a large tree that was planted in the front yard, surrounded by a freshly mowed lawn. I took a mental photo for my memory in case this would be the only time I'd see it.

"What are you waiting for sis, go meet your daddy," Alex said, pushing me toward the door.

"Ok I'm going, I'll be back to get you." I took a deep breath, stepped out the car and walked across the street. The closer I got to the door, the more anxious I became. My palms were clammy, my stomach was churning, my body broke out into a cold sweat and my heart felt it was going to jump out of my chest. I quickly wiped my face and hands before reaching the doorstep.

I rang the bell.

Ding Dong.

No answer. I waited a few seconds before I rang it again.

Ding Dong.

Two minutes went by, still no answer. I turned to walk away with tears building in my eyes, when a masculine voice called out, "Who is it?"

I turned around quick. "Hello, is Mr. Mitchell available, sir?"

"Who wants to know and why?"

"Sir, I don't mean any harm or disrespect but it is imperative that I speak with Mr. Mitchell only, regarding a sensitive and personal matter."

I was getting a little annoyed with mystery man behind the door and his disregard for this emergency matter.

"What is your name young lady?"

"Tonya sir, my name is Tonya."

If he asked another damn question I was sure to lose my cool. The door cracked open first, then a tall, handsome, well-groomed man appeared.

"Tonya? My daughter, Tonya?"

Looking into his face was like looking at my own. The resemblance was incredible, from the almond shape eyes to the uniquely shaped nose.

"If your name is Quentrell Mitchell, than yes, I am your daughter."

"Well I'll be damned, I thought I'd never find you!"

Without warning he grabbed me up in a tight bear-like hug. I cried like a newborn baby in his arms...I'd found my dad...I finally have *real* dad.

CHAPTER THIRTEEN

NEW BEGINNINGS

ALEX

I was so happy that I could be here for my girl. I just prayed everything would work out for her. She didn't need any more disappointments than what life had already dealt her. Shadow and I were lighting it up like we lived in Jamaica as we waited for her. I watched her as she walked to the door and after a few minutes when no one answered I thought the worst had happened. When I saw her coming back toward the car I said, "Shit!" Then I saw her turn around. I took a pull of the spliff and damn near chocked to death when this man came from behind the door. I'd have to wait until their hug ended to see his face clearly. When he stood up straight, I felt like my lungs collapsed and all the air was sucked out of me. I jumped out the car and made a mad dash across the street.

TONYA

"Why are you crying babygirl?" he asked, wiping away his own tears.

"Words can't express how happy I am right now," I said, reaching around his waist for another hug.

"I am just as happy," he said, tightening his hold.

"Daddy? What are you doing here? What's going on? Both of us turned around, shocked to see Alex standing there, him more than me.

"What are you doing Alex? I told you I would come to get you."

"Alexandria? Is that you? What the hell are you doing out here?"

This whole scene was throwing me for a loop.

"Excuse my French but, how the hell do you know my best friend? Alex why are you calling him Daddy? Please tell me you two haven't slept together."

Neither one of them responded.

"Well don't both of y'all answer at once."

Alex was the one to break the staring contest they'd become locked in. "No, I didn't sleep with him Tonya.

This is my father Keith."

"Ugh I think your mistaken Alex, his name is Quentrell Mitchell not Keith Williams," I said looking at my father for clarity.

"This is crazy. I think you ladies should come in," he said, walking into the house.

Alex and I both just stood there with our mouths wide open, this was going to be an interesting day. The interior of his home was even more immaculate then the outside.

As he gave us a tour of his lovely home, I noticed a lot of pictures of him, Alex and her brothers on the walls. There were two beautiful chandeliers that seemed to just call out to you. One hung at the bottom of a long, winding staircase and another over a marble top table with a solid wood crafted base and eight chairs. The entire house was painted in a glossy maroon color. There were five bedrooms, three bathrooms, an arcade in the basement, a theater room, and a miniature gym. The living room was almost as big as my entire apartment.

"Ladies please have a seat. Would you like something to drink?"

We both declined.

"Dad, when did you move here?" Alex asked.

"A few months ago," our dad answered.

I interjected, "So where do we begin?".

"Let's start with how you two met," he said, pointing to both Alex and me.

"We went to elementary school together, things weren't always this cool between us but eventually we became friends and have been close ever since," I said, wrapping my arm around Alex's shoulder.

"Now you tell us how you could be both Keith and Quentrell," Alex shot his way.

KEITH

I knew that one was coming ."Uh ok. Back in the day when I was a big time hustler in Arizona, I met your mother, Alexandria. I was getting money out there but like people say 'too much of something is good for nothing'. I got caught up with some people down there and some things popped off. Your mother and I packed your brothers up and relocated to New York. When we moved to New York, I created new identities for me and her.

I was now Quentrell Mitchell and she became Patricia Mitchell. It wasn't long before I established a name for myself in the city. With the new image and money also came the females. I'd never cheated on your mother before and I didn't intend to. But there was this one female who was so persistent. Tasha McMillan. She was as pretty as they came, but it wasn't her looks that snagged me, it was her determination.

One night my crew and I went out to splurge at the *Golden Lady*. When we arrived, Tasha stepped on the stage. I didn't even know she was a dancer. She was doing her thing onstage, then she just stopped and ran off. I had the bouncer bring her back and we hit it off from there.

Four months later, Patricia approached me about the rumored affair. I had never lied to her in the past and I wasn't about to start, so I told the truth. She gave me an ultimatum—end the affair or she would end our child's life. I thought she lost her mind for a second. I asked her what the hell was wrong with her and why she would threaten our children's lives. That's when she took my hand and placed it on her belly.

I had been in the street so much that I hadn't noticed Patricia was sporting a small baby bump. After that day, I left Tasha alone. Two months later she left town. About six months later, I bumped into her sister Laura in the supermarket. Laura told me that Tasha had given birth prematurely to a babygirl. I started to give my condolences when Laura cut me short and told me that the baby was not only alive and well but that she was mine.

I couldn't believe it. I was furious with Tasha. She had to have known she was pregnant before she left. How could she not tell me? I had to be the one to break this news to Patricia. I rushed home that night but when I got there she was already gone as well as the boys. All that was left was a letter on her pillow. In the letter it said that she'd heard the rumor and that was the final straw.

It was one thing for me to cheat on her but to get another woman pregnant was something she couldn't deal with. She said she was taking the kids and this was goodbye forever.

"So, Tonya is the rumored love child?

"Yes, that's right Alexandria. Tonya is your older sister. Three weeks after Patricia left, I got the call from her mother saying that she was in labor. Despite Patricia's request for me not to come, I made it my business to be there. I then was the father of two sons and two daughters."

"Why didn't you come looking for me after you found out? Tonya asked.

"Babygirl, I've been looking for you for sixteen years. When you were about four I think, I heard your mom had moved back in town. I didn't know where to look for you until I saw Laura again. She gave me a Bronx address for y'all. When I knocked on the door, some dude answered. Not sure if I had the right apartment or not, I asked to speak to Tasha. Dude asked me who I was and what was my business with Tasha. I told him I was your father and the nigga got disrespectful and told me he was your father. I punched that mother fucker right in his mouth. We were tussling in the hall when your mom came off the elevator with you by her side. She ran over to his side and I picked you up. Holding you in my arms, there was no doubt that you were mine.

Tasha ran up on me, snatched you out my arms and told me to never come back around. I didn't want to deal with her ignorance. I knew one day I would be able to get to you.

Do you remember the man who use to give you money for the icy man?"

"Yea! That was my first grade year! How did you know about that man?"

I laughed lightly. "That man was me babygirl. That was the only way I was able to see you. When y'all moved again, I couldn't find you. After five years and no luck, I had nothing but faith to rely on. I knew that one day we'd find one another somehow."

ALEX

"This is crazy! All this time we've been close like sisters and you were really my sister. Wow, stuff like this only happens in movies and books," I said to Tonya. I got up and hugged her. "I couldn't have asked for a better sister, wait I take that back…maybe one who didn't cry so much." I laughed and Tonya punched me in the arm. Something hit me and I had to sit for a second. "Dad do you remember that friend I was telling you about?" Tonya shot me a dirty look. I knew I was going to hear it later from her but I didn't care.

"Which one? The girl with devil for a father? Yea I reme… Oh God No! No! Please tell me it wasn't you Tonya that Alexandria has been telling me about Please!" Our father yelled and cried at the same time.

"Yes it was me but Alex wasn't supposed to tell you. Alex you promised!"

"I promised that nothing would happen to him at the hands of my fa… our father and I kept that promise," I said trying to defend myself.

"I'm sorry Alexandria but that's another promise

broken because that man's days are limited now!" our father yelled.

"Please Dad, just leave it alone, he's not worth it! I just got you in my life and I don't want to lose you for some bullshit!" Tonya pleaded.

TONYA

I'm going to kill Alex for running her big mouth. Now here I was pleading with our father to think about the bright future ahead. "Just promise me you'll leave it alone, Dad." I watched as he paced the floor.

"Ok, I'll leave him alone but *only* because you asked me too."

"This has been one crazy day and I am tired. Alex are you ready to go home."

"Yes sis, this has been a lonngg day, let's go home."

"Dad, I'm so glad I got to meet you. I can't wait to spend more time with you. Let's not lose contact ever again, please," I said, giving him my cell number. Leaving his house, I felt like a weight had been lifted off my shoulders. I fell asleep listening to Alex tell Shadow everything that happened inside.

When I awoke, we were parked in front of Ronnie's.

"Yo what the fuck is this about?" I said, popping up. I did not want to see that nigga and I thought my sister would have known this.

"Calm down sis, Ronnie called while he was driving

back and told Shadow to come pick something up."

"Well I hope he hurries up because I don't wanna see that scandalous ass nigga."

As soon as his named rolled off my tongue, he walked out the house with Shadow.

"You got to be fucking kidding me, what the fuck man!" I wanted to be anywhere but in the car at that moment.

"What's up Alex?" Ronnie said, reaching for the car door.

"He's not getting in this car, is he?"

"Relax shorty, his car is getting detailed. I'm just giving him a ride to shop," Shadow said, nonchalantly.

"Yo, Alex are you fucking serious right now? Let me out please," I said, trying to unlock the door.

"Sis, it's going to be a quick ride, plus you don't know shit about traveling in Brooklyn."

She was right about that. Whenever we came out here we were in the car. "This is some real bullshit but it's whatever!"

Ronnie got in, I said nothing. Before he even closed the door he started, "I see you still wearing your ring, I guess you're not that mad at me."

It was a little too soon for the wise cracks. I took my left hand with the ring, swung and connected with his jaw. I knocked the shit out of him. When he tried to block my punch, he must've forgotten he didn't close his door and leaned back. He fell out the car. I started to jump on him but stopped short when I saw I was staring down the barrel of Shadow's locked and loaded .380.

"You lost your fucking mind bitch! Breathe the wrong way and I'll push your cap back!" Shadow said with the gun still pointed in my face.

"What the fuck babe, you're going crazy right now! Get that fucking gun out my sister's face!" Alex screamed.

RONNIE

Click Click

"Put the mother fucking gun down now Shadow or I'll splatter your fragments all over this bitch. Have you lost your fucking mind, putting a gun in my lady's face?"

"Yo, chill Ronnie, I was only looking out for you bro," Shadow said, putting his gun back in his waste.

"Nigga, did I ask for your help? Huh? What her and I go through, is what we go through! Never get up in our shit again unless I say so! Are we clear on that?" I said, nudging him with Leana.

"Yea, we're clear," Shadow said, mouthing to me that I owed him as he got up.

The scene that just unfolded was an act, it was all planned. While they were on their way back, I called Shadow to check on him. Speaking in our code, he told me that Alex and Tonya were in the car with him. I told him to bring Tonya to me. When Shadow arrived we came up with the whole charade. I didn't know what I would say to upset her enough to swing on me but when I saw the ring, that was all the ammunition I needed. That girl could pack a punch though! I hadn't anticipated her hitting me that damn hard. But I'd taken a million of her hits if I had to, to get her to stay with me. I was hoping it wouldn't take that many though.

CHAPTER FOURTEEN

REUNITED

"**T**onya are you ok? I apologize on his behalf for that; he can get carried away sometimes. That's some left hook you got there girl"

"I'm not in the mood for jokes, Ronnie."

"Oh, so you do remember my name. I'm just kidding, come here girl."

"Nigga you gotta be kidding me," Tonya said, snarling.

I knew it wasn't going to be easy but I had to keep trying. "Ok let me stop with the jokes. On a serious note, would you come in the house and talk to me?"

I could see that she was hurt, felt betrayal and was disgusted. It was all in her eyes.

"Please Tonya," I added.

She hesitated but followed me reluctantly into house. For me that was progress, now all I had to do was get her to forgive me.

"What do you want Ronnie?" The hatred was thick in her tone.

"You," I answered honestly.

"I don't have time for the bullshit Ronnie, what the fuck do you really want?"

"I really do want you, Tonya."

"You want me, huh? So what about the bitch who's carrying your fucking *child*! Did you want me then too? Huh, motherfucker!" Tonya charged at me full speed.

I was trying to bob and weave her blows but her arms seemed to be moving at super human speed. She caught me with an upper cut that landed me flat on my ass. She jumped on me and started throwing haymakers. I didn't want to hit her so I just covered my face and let her take out her frustrations. As the blows slowed down, I could hear her crying and talking. "Why Ronnie, I gave you all of me. Was there something I didn't do?"

I felt her body lift off of mine. Unsure of her next move, I just laid there protecting my face. Her rants continued, "What? I didn't suck your dick enough?" She snatched my pants off, dropped down to her knees and took my dick out of my pants. At this point I was kind of scared. I couldn't let her hurt the jewels.

"Babe what are you doi—"

"Shut the fuck up, you don't get to talk. Is this what you wanted?" she questioned, taking my dick into her mouth.

I should've been scared but her mouth was so warm and felt so good that it deactivated my common sense sensor. I went to grab her head.

"Don't fucking touch me. I bet you don't have to guide her fucking head," she said as she started sucking my dick extra fast. "Oh no, maybe her pussy was tighter than mine, on second thought I doubt that. Maybe she worked her pussy better."

Before I could respond she lifted her skirt and climbed on top of me.

"Na, I bet she can't ride this dick better than me, right...right?"

The way she was gyrating her hips and her walls were massaging me, I could feel myself getting ready to let off a load. I don't know if it was out of fear or because she'd just laid the pussy down. She knew she'd taken me there and then she stopped.

She looked at me with this devilish grin and said, "That's what I thought, that bitch can't fuck you like I can. I'm done with this shit Ronnie, don't come looking for me."

With that said, she stood up and tried to walk away like nothing happened. I couldn't let that shit happen like that. I grabbed her leg and brought her down, if she wanted to play rough then that's how we would play.

"Get off me Ronnie," she screamed, trying to fight me off. I locked her arms together, forced her legs open and pushed myself into her.

"Get off me Rooonniiee." Her demands turned into soft moans as I hit that G-spot up. "Ugh I hatttee yoouu

Ronniiee."

"But I love you," I said as stroked her gently.

"Uugghh shiitt! I hatte you! I swearrrr I doo."

The orgasm that was building was stronger than the hate she was feeling. "You may hate me but this pussy loves me…ummm, listen to her sing my name."

Her pussy was so wet; the sounds of my dick sliding into her tight canal mixed with the sounds of her pussy farting made beautiful music together.

"I know you still love me because I still love you, Tonya. I'm sorry for hurting you baby and I'll never do it again, I promise you." I spoke these words into her ear as one of her biggest orgasms she's ever had rocked her to the core of her body. Feeling her juices dripping down my shaft caused me to release too. Tonya was crying hysterically as her body continued to release her essence.

"Please don't hurt me again Ronnie, please." She cried into my shoulder.

"I swear, I will never hurt you again as long as I live." I picked her up and carried her into the shower. I washed and caressed her body. When I was done rinsing her, I dried and lotioned her. I helped her get dressed but when she went to walk out the door, I practically begged her to stay.

"Where are you going Tonya?"

"I'm going home Ronnie"

"Why don't you come back here? This is your home?"

"It's too soon Ronnie, I need more time."

"You said you forgave me, Tonya."

"I do Ronnie but I need more time to get my thoughts

together."

"What else is there to think about Tonya?"

"You're going to be a father in a few months Ronnie and I am not the expecting mother. I need to think this through, I need to figure out if I'm going to be able to handle this. I'll get back to you in a couple of days with my decision. I love you, Ronnie."

Those were her final words as she walked out the house.

TONYA

I didn't know it was possible to love someone more than you love yourself until that moment. I couldn't picture my life with out him, no matter how hard I tried. I truly loved Ronnie in every sense of the word. When I told him I forgave him, my decision was already made. I would accept his love child and love it as my own because I loved its father and everything about him.

I was going to string him along for awhile though, because I couldn't allow him to think he'd gotten over that easy. What he did, damn near destroyed me but I would accept his flaws, just like he did mine.

When I got in the car Shadow starting apologizing immediately. I told him that I completely understood and for him not to worry about it. Truth be told, I would've done the same thing if I thought Alex was in trouble.

By the time I got back to my mother's house, I was

exhausted, mentally and physically. I wanted to crawl in bed and not wake up until the next evening. As I climbed in my bed, my mother walked into the room.

"I need to talk to you about something."

"Not right now Mommy, I'm tired. It's been a long day."

"This is important, Tonya." She stood her ground.

"Ugghh! What is so important that it couldn't wait 'til morning?"

"Read this," she said, tossing me a letter from Rikers.

"Ma, I know you're not keeping me awake to read a letter from Richard after I told you I was beat."

"Just read!" she yelled.

I saw that her body was trembling so I knew something was wrong. After reading Richard's letter, I knew why she was so shaken up. In the letter, he used gory details to describe how he'd been robbed of his manhood. He said that he was now contemplating suicide because he couldn't live like this. At the end of the letter he addressed me directly, by name, asking for me to please help him.

"What am I supposed to do Mom?"

"Get him out of jail." She answered with such confidence.

"What! How am I supposed to do that? This ain't Monopoly Mom. I can't present a *Get Out of Jail Free* card and they just release him. Secondly why should I? After all the shit he did to me and I'm supposed to turn the other cheek?"

"I knew your were going to be difficult. Listen, the boys need their father. It hasn't been easy trying to raise them on my own. I'm not asking you to forgive him or forget what he's done, I'm just asking you think about your brothers. They're suffering without him and I know what he did to you was fucked up but I know you Tonya, and your heart is not that cold babygirl."

"If I help him what's in it for me?"

"If you retract your story and he's successfully released, we'll get to be a family again minus the bullshit. Don't you miss the trips, family outings, the feeling of being a whole family unit."

I looked at my mother with total disbelief. Did she really try to play me with that family bullshit? I had something for her ass. "I did at one time but those things mean nothing to me now. I have all the family I'll ever need. But, I'm going to help him for my brothers sake because they are young and don't understand. As far as me being part of that *happy family picture*...you can dead it! I want no part of that. After he's released, that will be my last tie to you. How dare you try to use the family card, when we both know his release is more for your personal satisfaction than anything else. If that man is worth you selling your soul, then you will burn on your own."

"This is for all us Tonya. Everything is going to work out fine, you'll see," she said as she stood to leave. When she saw me doing the same she stopped. "Where do you think you're going at this time of night?"

"I agreed to help you right, so what I do from now on, is none of your business."

With that said, I grabbed my bags and left. I called

Ronnie when I got downstairs. He said he was in the area and would be here in ten minutes.

RONNIE

I knew her call would come, though I didn't expect it this soon but I was more that happy that it did. My heart warmed at the thought that she still felt comfortable enough in her time of need to call me. Once I got her home, I planned on showing her how much I really missed and loved her. When I pulled up out front, she was sitting on the steps with her bags. I quickly put all her stuff in the trunk and helped her into the car.

I looked at her as the car's lights bounced off her eyes. Her face was so beautiful, her skin so smooth and radiant; it had sort of a glow to it. She was simply gorgeous and I couldn't wait to make her my wife. I pulled off with the thoughts of our future fresh in my mind. Before we got home, she passed out in the car. Not wanting to disturb my sleeping beauty, I picked her up and carried her into the house. When I was crossing the threshold, her grip tightened around my neck.

I placed small little kisses on her forehead as I took her upstairs and placed her in the bed. After closing the door, I walked down the hall to check on Candie. She was sleeping peacefully as well. After she told me about the pregnancy the other night, I had her pack her stuff and move into one of my guestrooms. I wanted to ensure the safety of my unborn child.

We agreed to remain strictly platonic with the signing of a *Friend Only* contract. After the delivery of our child she was to move into her own apartment, of her choice. I would pay all her bills—rent, utilities, cable and phone. All she would have to do is raise our child and she'd be taken care of for life. Any breech of the *Friend Only* contract on her end, she'd be on her own.

Now she knew that Tonya would eventually be coming home, but Tonya had no idea of this current arrangement. I prayed she'd go along with it and I was hoping the signed contract would show her that I was serious about us. I climbed in bed with the love of my life and fell into a comfortable slumber. When I awakened a few hours later she was gone.

TONYA

At 8:00 a.m. I was up and about I had a few things I had to take care of. My first stop was the DA's office. I wrote my retraction. The whole time Melody was in my ear asking if I sure I wanted to do this. She explained that it would be a four month process and that I was going to have to face the grand jury again. Accepting the terms, I signed it and walked out.

Before I could make it out the building, I had to run into the bathroom. After puking for the third time that morning, I started making my way to my second stop—

my GYN. I could feel something wasn't right, but I couldn't pinpoint it. Getting in a cab, my phone rang. It was Ronnie. "What's up baby?" I said into the phone.

"Nothing much. I woke up this morning and you were gone, is everything alright?"

"Yea, everything is fine. I have a doctor's appointment today."

"Oh ok, well how about I pick you up and we have lunch?"

"Sounds great. Meet me downtown at BBQ's by two, love you babe."

The cab pulled up in front of *Eastside Gynecology*. Looking at the time, I realized I was fifteen minutes early. I didn't have to wait long before being escorted back to the exam room. After speaking with the my doctor for a few minutes about my symptoms, she ordered a few test. Forty-Five minutes later, she came back.

CHAPTER FIFTEEN

PLAYING WITH FIRE

"Well Tonya," Dr. Michelle said, taking a seat. I'm afraid I don't have very good news today. First I guess a congratulations is in order. Your pregnancy test came back positive. So before you leave we'll do an ultrasound to determine how far along you are. Secondly, there is no easy way to say this...your HIV test came back positive. Before you freak out, during your vaginal I found that you had been infected with a serious case of Chlamydia which could be affecting the test result. So I'll also be drawing some blood today and the results will be back in three days. Do you have any questions for me?"

I must've shaken my head no because she left the room. Somewhere between pregnancy and HIV my mind blanked out and tuned back in when she said but and then blanked again when she said Chlamydia. How the fuck could this happen to me? Hadn't I suffered enough?

She came back in the room with the ultrasound machine. I laid down on the table and following her instructions, I scooted my butt far down. She used the vaginal probe first.

"Wow Tonya, when was your last menstrual?"

"On the 20th of this month, why Dr. Michelle?"

"Was it like your normal cycle?"

"Yes, I bled for four days. Why, what's wrong Dr. Michelle?" I asked, starting to get worried.

She pulled the probe out and put some gel on the lower part of my belly. "Well according to the size of your fetus, you are almost twenty weeks into the pregnancy."

"Ugh, you want to say that in English Dr. Michelle?"

"Tonya, you are almost five months pregnant.

"How could that be Dr. Michelle when I've been getting my menstrual every month?"

"What you have been experiencing is not a period but vaginal bleeding, which is common. This type of bleeding is usually very light, but it can sometimes seem like an actual period. A lot of women report that they bleed regularly during the early portion of their pregnancies. Vaginal bleeding is often referred to as early pregnancy bleeding and is caused by hormonal changes in the body due to the pregnancy."

"So should I be worried?"

"No, not all," she said, turning the screen my way.

Immediately, I started to cry when I saw my baby moving its arms and legs.

"Oh my God, there is really a baby in there," I said, ecstatically.

"Yes, there is. Would you like to know the sex of the baby?"

"You can tell me that now?"

"I sure can, would you like to know?"

"Yes…yes please Dr. Michelle!"

"It's a girl! Congratulations Tonya!"

I was too happy to speak so I just laid there and let the tears of joy fall from my eyes. Thirty minutes later I was out of there with my prescriptions and sonogram. I got to the BBQ's restaurant at 2:15 p.m. This was sure to be an interesting lunch date. When I got there Ronnie already had my favorite appetizer waiting.

"Hey baby," I said, giving him a kiss.

"Hey babe, how was your doctor's appointment?"

"Interesting would be an understatement," I said.

"Oh yea, what happened that was so interesting?" Ronnie chuckled.

I wanted to smack the smile right off his face but I kept my cool. "What do you want first, the good or the bad news?"

"Give me the good news first, I'm in a good mood."

I passed him the sonogram backwards. On it I had written, *Our Daughter*.

"Is this for real ma?"

"Turn it around and you'll see our babygirl."

Turning the picture over, the biggest grin spread

across his face.

"This is for real? You're really going to have my daughter?" He got up and picked me up in the middle of the restaurant. Everybody turned to see what the commotion was about. Ronnie, not ashamed of this news yelled, "She's having my daughter!"

The nosy people around us applauded and congratulated us on our new addition.

RONNIE

"Oh man, my baby is having my baby! Today is a good day."

I could tell something was wrong because it was written all her face.

"What's wrong babe, you should be happy right now."

"I am happy Ronnie but did you forget I said there was some bad news too?" she said getting closer.

In the midst of my celebration, I'd forgotten she had something else to tell me.

"Well go ahead babe, what else is there for you to tell me?"

"Ronnie I'm not sure yet but I might have HIV. What I know for sure is that you gave me Chlamydia."

"What the fuck are you talking about Tonya? Have you been fucking around on me because I ain't never been burnt!

Smaacck! She slapped the shit out of me. I deserved that, plus more. I knew she'd never fucked around on me but I'd rather place the blame on her then admit again that I fucked up.

"I'm sorry Tonya, I know it wasn't you. I'm sorry that I keep fucking your life up. I'm sorry I wasn't a better man but baby I'm going to make this work…I gotta go."

I got up, dropped some money on the table and left. I called Candie as soon as I got in the car.

"Hello."

"Ayo bitch! Are you fucking burning?" I screamed into the phone.

"What the fuck are you talking about Ronnie, my test results all came back negative. You better check your other bitches, you nasty nigga. *Click.* She hung up the phone.

"Dammnnitt!" I yelled. I had to sit back and think hard, about who I'd fucked in the past year.

Nooo! It couldn't have been her, she wouldn't do me like that, but it had to be her…she was the only other person I fucked.

"What's up Ronnie?"

"Bitch, don't what's up me! You fucking burnt me!"

"Ahahaha nigga! You're just now finding out. If you're going to be stepping out on your lady, then you should be doing two things…strapping up and getting your equipment checked out every three months!"

"You're dead Alex! I promise you that…on my unborn children's lives. Tonya will be burying her sister."

"Fuck you Ronnie, you don't scare me nigga!"

TONYA

I couldn't believe that nigga had the nerve to accuse me of doing the creeping. Punk ass nigga, instead of being a man and owning his shit, he pulled a coward move. Since I was almost uptown, I called Alex. She forwarded my call to voicemail. I guess she was busy so I left a message.

"Hey sis call me, I got some good news." I ended the call and decided to go home.

When I got home, I heard the shower running upstairs.

"Well damn, if you were coming home you could've given me a ride," I said stripping down. When I opened the shower, I got the shock of my life when I saw the girl who crashed my party standing in my shower. I snatched a towel. "Bitch are you dumb, stupid or crazy? What the fuck are you doing in my house?" I shouted in her face.

"I live here bitch or didn't Ronnie tell you?" she snorted.

"What the fuck do you mean by you live here?"

"Call your man shorty and question him."

I didn't want to believe this bitch. I didn't think he'd have the balls or heart to hurt me again. I picked up the house phone and dialed his number, he answered on the third ring.

"Yea, what is it Candie?"

"Oh so this bitch is telling the truth? Fuck you Ronnie."

RONNIE

Oh shit, during lunch with all the bombshells being dropped, I didn't have the time to tell Tonya about Candie. "Tonya just calm down for a second and let me explain."

"Explain what Ronnie? It's pretty much self explanatory. I come home and she's here and she said to ask you what she was doing here. I call your cell and you call me Candie, confirming that you did know she was here. Did I miss something?"

"Stay there, I'm on my way!"

"Better make it quick or I'm going to whip on this chick."

I jumped on the BQE doing seventy miles per hour. I got home in twenty minutes.

"Tonya and Candie," I hollered up the stairs, "Get down here now!"

I went into my office and grabbed the signed and notarized copy of the contract. By the time I got back to the living room, both ladies where sitting on opposite ends of the sectional. I chose to address Tonya first.

"Tonya, I assumed by you coming back that meant you accepted the fact that I will be having a child with Candie. Was I right?"

"Yes, Ronnie but I don't see what that has to do with her living here?"

"I offered Candie a living arrangement for her and my child, upon her agreement to this contract that we signed," I said passing the contract to Tonya.

"Now Candie, when you signed that contract, you

knew there was a possibility that Tonya would becoming home. Am I right?"

"Yea, you're right."

"Ok, so now she's home and I expect you both to get along especially since she will be bearing the sister to our child in a few months."

"Excuse me? What did you say?"

"I said that Tonya will bear the sister to our child, meaning she is expecting as well, five months to be exact".

"This is fucking crazy! So you mean to tell me that we're both pregnant right now?"

"That's exactly what I'm saying. Tonya is about two months further along than you but yes, y'all will both be bearing my children. This is not how I pictured things to be but this is what it is. I'm just trying to make the best of it. In the mean time I will try to make y'all both as comfortable as possible during your transitions into motherhood."

"Tonya are you ok with the contract and these current living arrangements?"

"I guess I have no choice but to be, as long as she doesn't breech this contract, I'll be fine."

"Ok, Candie will you be ok with these current living arrangements?"

"It's a lot to take in Ronnie, but yea I'll be fine."

"I'm glad we were able to come together as adults. I say we got out to celebrate."

"You're pushing it now Ronnie," Tonya said, playfully shoving me.

"Hey, it was worth a shot," I joked.

"Get your orders together so I can call and get dinner delivered. I need to make a phone call. I went into my office and called one of my other hit men, Butch. I informed him this was a very special mission that he could never speak on again after this conversation. I gave him my mark's name, address and detailed instructions on how I wanted the kill done.

TONYA

Over the next three months, things began to really to pick up. When my test results for the HIV came back negative, I dropped to my knees and thanked the Lord above. When I told Alex about her niece, she was ecstatic. We came up with the name together, Sariyah Patrice Jackson. Then I finally told her about him burning me, she was so apologetic.

She kept saying, "Oh I'm so sorry, I'm so sorry."

I told her to shut up. The way she kept apologizing, you would've thought she was the one who burnt me. During this time, Candie and I started to become close. I was with her when she found out that she was expecting a little boy. Ronnie had his pair on the way and he couldn't have been happier. He turned two of the guestrooms into nurseries—one pink and one blue. Candie and I did all the shopping for both rooms together. Because things were going so smooth, Candie decided she would stay here with us after Rondell Jr. was born. This way he'd be closer to his sister and to make it easier on Ronnie's pockets.

I visited my dad twice. The first time I went to tell him about the pregnancy face to face. At first he was upset like any parent would be but when I told him it was a little girl, he was ready for her to come out on the spot. He asked me where Alex was and I explained I hadn't seen her much lately. I guess she and Shadow were spending a lot of quality time together.

The second visit he wanted to meet the man who captured his daughter's heart. When they met, my dad almost had a heart attack. When I asked what was wrong, he said that Ronnie was a splitting image of his father. Both Ronnie and I were shocked to find out that our fathers use to run together back in the day. My dad instantly took a liking to Ronnie. They traded stories about the drug game, past and present.

Ronnie even confided in my dad about Candie and me both being pregnant. My dad wasn't mad and told us that he would help us with anything we needed. I was still in charge of tallying the money but that was now done at home. I would still go to the Tiphani's every three weeks for my regular wash & set and monthly gossip. Champagne was still as crazy as ever but I didn't expect anything less from him.

The reappearance ticket, for me to take the stand in front of the grand jury came up quicker than the DA had anticipated.

Today Ronnie, Candie and Shadow were here with me. Alex hadn't showed up or answered any of our calls.

She would definitely hear my mouth when I saw her. An hour on the stand and the jury decided to drop all charges. As I walked of out the courtroom Richard walked up to me and attempted to hug me.

Ronnie started to reach for him but I told him I had this one. "Don't ever come near me or my child again because if you do, that man across the street will handle you himself," I said pointing to my father.

Richard and my mother both looked like they'd seen a ghost when they looked in the direction I was pointing.

"Yea Mom, I forgot to tell you; I found my Dad...my real Dad."

I walked away that day, leaving that part of my life behind me with my head held high.

"I'm proud of you," Ronnie said, helping me into the car. We were on our way home from dinner, when Ronnie got a 911 text from Shadow. Since he was driving I made the call.

"Hey Shadow, it's me Tonya, What's up?"

"That mother fucker killed her, he killed my fucking life."

"Whoa, wait slow down, slow down. Who killed who?" I asked, trying to get him to calm down and make sense of what he was saying while putting him on speaker so Ronnie could listen.

"Alex left me for another nigga a few weeks ago. She left me a letter saying that she found someone that made her happier. She packed all her things and left a plane ticket stub on my pillow, with a destination to the Bahamas. I was too embarrassed to say anything.

I figured she would've told you by now, that's why I haven't been around much. Anyway about an hour after I got home tonight, someone rang my doorbell. When I got to the door, there was no one there but one of Alex's suitcases.

I figured she was just trying to hurt me so I dragged the bag and left it in the corner. I sat in a chair across from the bag and just stared at it for a few hours. After a few shots of Henny, curiosity got the best of me. When I opened the bag, my world ended. In the suitcase was Alex's body chopped into several pieces and frozen in zip lock bags. The police are on the way now. Tell Ronnie I need him!"

"Aaaahhhhh…ahhhhh…ahhhhh," I started screaming. My screaming startled Ronnie and he swerved into an 18 wheeler on the opposite side of the lane. As Ronnie tried to regain control of the car, we crashed into a guard-rail and our car started flipping over and over again, then…darkness.

CHAPTER SIXTEEN

REALITY CHECK

TONYA

When I opened my eyes, the combination of sirens from an ambulance and the flashing lights from police cars were making my head throb. I tried to look around to see where all the noise was coming from, but I only saw the feet of people and tires of a car. *Why is everything upside down?* I tried to move several times before I realized that my upper body was pinned to the seat by a deployed airbag.

"What the hell is going on?" I muttered out. Flashes of

our car flipping over began to replay like a movie scene.

"Ronnie! Roonniee!" I screamed. Looking over towards the driver's seat, there were shards of glass sticking out of Ronnie's face, his head was pressed against the steering wheel and his eyes had an eerie dead stare in them. I reached out and grabbed his wrist, I began to feel for a pulse…nothing. "No Ronnie! No baby, please! You can't leave like this, what about Jr. and Sari…" During all the commotion, I'd forgotten about my babygirl.

Instinctively, I rubbed my stomach and she didn't move which was abnormal for her. I shook my stomach roughly, up and down then side to side and still nothing. A gush of warm fluid flowed down my legs. I knew I didn't piss on myself. I reached between my legs and pulled my hand from under my dress. I panicked when I saw blood. I began to feel light-headed and felt myself drifting away. The next time I opened my eyes, I was lying in a hospital bed.

Next to my bed was Alex, sitting in a white chair wearing a beautiful white sundress and holding Sariyah in her arms. It must have been a bad dream. I said to myself.

"She's beautiful sis! Y'all did a good job," Alex said, smiling.

"Tell the truth, I don't even remember giving birth sis," I laughed.

"I told you that you were crazy," Alex said, bursting into cheerful laughter.

I turned my head and gazed out of the window. "It's beautiful outside today," I said observing the clear blue sky, the beautiful white clouds and bright shining sun.

"Yea, we always have the best weather here," Alex said, still smiling down at Sariyah.

"Girl, I don't know what you're talking about. You know we rarely get good weather like this, especially around this time of year."

Alex burst into disturbing laughter this time. "Sis the weather here is always beautiful, where do you think you're at, New York?" She doubled over in laughter.

"Uh, yea bitch!" I chuckled. "You been smoking that shit again?" I said jokingly but staring at her seriously.

"Girl bye, I can't be bothered with you." Alex looked down at her watch. "Oh snap, it's time to go."

"Where are we going? Shopping? That would be cool, I need to get more stuff for Sariyah anyway."

"Girl you're a comedian today. It's that time, now come on, don't get left," Alex said, walking toward the room door.

I was really starting to worry about my sister. I think she was beginning to lose her mind. "Sis whatever you was smoking, don't buy that shit no more. It's got you tweaking," I said, reaching for Sariyah.

"Sis it's time to go now. You want to stay here that's on you but me and Sariyah are out."

Now I knew this bitch was bugging if she thought she was taking my daughter. "Iight sis, I don't know what you're on but you're not taking my daughter anywhere. Give me Sariyah," I said, jumping out of the bed and walking toward her.

"Tonya what is wrong with you, it's time to go; we

Marie A. Norfleet

can come back tomorrow damn."

When I reached the hallway and looked down the hall in the direction Alex was walking, there was a lighted path with a ray of white light beaming down.

"What is going on Alex, give my daughter to me now!" I said, reaching for Sariyah again.

"Sis we've been called, it's time to go!" Alex said, walking toward the bright light with my babygirl in her arms.

"Called where? Go where Alex? Your ass is really tripping. Give my daughter to me and don't call me until you get your mind right," I said, running up on her. When I went to snatch her arm, to make her turn around and face me, I grabbed air.

"What the fuck is going on Alex?" I started crying and back away. She finally turned to face me. I didn't recognize her anymore. Her face was sliced up beyond recognition.

"It's time to go sis, they're waiting on us."

"They? Who Alex? What the fuck happened to your face?"

"I'll explain once we cross over to the other side."

As Alex turned back around, I saw what appeared to be wings unfolding from her dress. I broke down hysterically crying at that point; it was now becoming clear to me what she'd been trying to tell me.

"No Alex, it's neither one of our time to go!" I screamed. Alex never turned back around, she kept walking with Sariyah tucked securely in her arms.

"Noooo Alex, please don't do this, she's just a baby!

She hasn't experienced life yet. Please Alex! Noooo!" I yelled frantically as Alex waved her final goodbye before walking directly into the ray of light.

"Tonyaaa baby, come back to me! Tonyaaa!" I heard a familiar female voice calling my name as she shook my body.

"Alex Nooo!" I screamed and jumped up. When I looked around the room, my eyes connected with my mother's, who was sitting by my beside. I grabbed at my stomach, it was soft.

"She stole my daughter Ma, she stole my babygirl!" I tried to jump out of the bed but the pain hit me and stopped that instantly. I fell back onto the bed. "Ma, why are you just sitting there? You have to go get help! Alex stole your granddaughter. She's wearing a white sundress…she couldn't have gotten that far."

My mother didn't budge. Instead, she just sat in the same white chair Alex had been sitting in and cried. "What the hell…didn't you hear what I just said? That crazy bitch stole your grandchild and you're just sitting there. Unfucking believable!"

"It's going to be alright Tonya," my mother said with a strained voice.

"Please tell me how it will be alright Ma when she stole your grandchild and you let her do it."

My mother started balling. "Alex couldn't have stole Sariyah because Alex is dead Tonya! She's dead!"

First Alex, now my mother was acting crazy. "What the fuck? Did you and Alex smoke that bullshit together. What the hell is wrong with y'all?"

My mother grabbed the remote and turned the TV on and oh my God she wasn't lying. Every news channel had a picture of Alex and they all said it in their own way but the message was clear, Alex was gone.

"Why!" was all that would be heard from my room for the rest of the night. I woke up the next morning with a splitting headache. I couldn't believe that someone took my sister away from me. "Ahhh whyyy!" I screamed out loud and my hand brushed my stomach. That's when I remembered that my babygirl was still missing. Quick flashes of the car flipping over flashed before my eyes and I remembered the horrific accident. "Oh nooo nooo nooo! Not my daughter too! She's all I had left."

A doctor rushed into my room. "Ms. Arlington you have to calm down or you'll bust your stitches. What's the problem?"

"My daughter is gooonnee," I cried.

"Gone? Gone where Ms. Arlington?"

"Sariyah, my daughter Sariyah is dead." My body was now shaking violently as I spoke those unbelievable words.

"Ms. Arlington, I am happy to tell you that Sariyah is just fine."

I couldn't believe my ears. "How is that even possible Dr…? Excuse me what is your name."

"I'm Dr. Bryan O'Neil and you, young lady are very lucky to be alive. By the grace of God there was an ambulance getting ready to get off the exit when your car flipped over. They rushed you here to Bard Hall Hospital in Brooklyn, where we were able to perform an emergency C-section. Sariyah was touch and go at first, but now she's stable."

"Thank you so much Dr. O'Neil, how I can ever repay you?"

"If you want to repay me, then you will relax and let your body heal." He turned to leave.

"Uh, Dr. O'Neil," I called out for his attention.

"Yes Ms. Arlington," Dr. O'Neil said, turning back to face me.

"There was a guy i—"

He cut me short. "Mr. Jackson is in critical but stable condition. He's suffering from a hairline fracture as well as multiple contusions. He will mostly like need plastic surgery to correct some of the damage done to his face."

"It's that bad Dr. O'Neil?" I asked, trying not to envision the damage.

"That is my medical opinion, but I am also a man of faith. His full recovery is on our Father's hands. I, along with a team of specialist, am just his tools to aide in the process."

"I understand Dr. O'Neil. One last question, when will I be able to see my daughter?"

"I would prefer that you wait until you're able to stand with minimal pain but I understand the need to see your daughter. I'll have a nurse come with a wheelchair when you're ready."

"Thank you, Dr. O'Neil for everything."

"Please call me Bryan, Dr. O'Neil was my father's name."

"Okay, Bryan it is, but thank you again."

"No need to thank me, it's not only my job but my pleasure to help. I'll be in later to check on you."

I let my body relax and drifted off to sleep. I dreamt of Alex for the third time that day. I was awakened about three hours later by a stocky unfriendly nurse.

"Wake up! Let's go! Stupid ass little girl."

The last part I don't think I was suppose to hear. "Excuse me?" I said, wiping the sleep from my eyes.

"You young girls make me sick, babies having babies. What the hell is this world coming too?"

This chick had to be off her meds or something because she couldn't be serious talking to me like that.

"When did my age become any of your business? You're supposed to be transporting me to the NICU to see my child, not ridiculing me. Now do your job and know that I'll be in touch with your superior."

"I'm sorry, Ms. Arlington. I'll have you to your daughter in no time," she said, helping me into the wheelchair. It amused me how quick her demeanor changed at the mention of contacting her boss.

Though my mother was a piece of work most of the time, she did teach me a few lessons that would stick with me forever. Case in point, how to fight ignorance with intelligence. I sat back and enjoyed the ride, thinking about what it would be like to see and hold my daughter for the first time. A feeling of anxiety mixed with excitement came over me as we finally made it to the exterior doors of the Neonatal Intensive Care Unit. After scrubbing down, I was finally allowed into the nursery.

The sight of the premature babies on life support

machines broke me down. I cried even worse when I reached Sariyah's bed and saw she had a two prong mask on with tubes in her nose, a tube down her throat, an IV in her left hand and a long tube coming out of the right side of her chest.

"What is all this crap? Why does she have so many tubes?" I yelled out.

I was quickly approached by an elderly black woman.

"Your daughter is a fighter just like you."

"Fighter? Like me? What do you mean? Do I know you?"

"Pardon me dear child, where are my manners. My name is Estelle and I'm one of your daughter's nurses here in the NICU. The reason I say she's a fighter like you is because I worked for Northern Hospital about two years ago. I was one of your nurses, in the trauma unit, that night you were brought in. When I saw you being rushed in here last night, I started praying for you immediately.

I was called into the operating room fifteen minutes later to assist with the delivery. Ten minutes later, while prepping for the surgery, we discovered that the baby was in distress. Once the bag was cut open, the presence of Meconium was found. Three minutes later, she was pulled from your womb but the worst was confirmed... she wasn't breathing. After six minutes of working on her, they were ready to give up until Dr. O'Neil said, 'No! Keep working on her.'

God is so good, let me tell you because two minutes later she let out her first cry. I never doubted that she would pull through because her fight for life was identical to the fight I saw in you a short time ago."

As I listened to Estelle recall details of the encounters she had with me, I felt embarrassed that she'd seen me during such a horrific time in my life but strangely comforted at the same time, knowing that I had someone looking over me.

"Do you know why she has a tube coming out of her chest?"

"Once she got here in the NICU, the build of feces was so bad that it collapsed the air bubbles in her lungs. The tube was inserted to suction out the feces left in her, so that her lungs will function properly. If you need anything or have any more questions please feel free to ask and if I don't know the answer I will do my best to find someone who does," Ms. Estelle said while walking away to give me time with my babygirl.

My heart dropped into pit of my stomach as I got closer to her bed and got a good look at her. Looking at her in this condition tore me up and made me feel useless because I couldn't do anything to help her.

When I went to pick her up, another nurse in the unit rushed over and shouted at me that I couldn't hold her. Although I wanted to slap fire out of her for yelling at me, I had no choice but to understand that it was for Sariyah's safety. I sat at her bedside for hours until I dozed off. I was awakened to Ms. Nasty from earlier pushing me back to my room.

"We got off to a rough start earlier, my name is Joyce and I want to apologize for my outburst earlier. My daughter recently revealed her pregnancy and when I got your chart this morning, I realized that y'all were the same age and my personal anger spilled over into my job. That's no excuse for how I treated you and I'd really like to apologize."

I heard her but didn't respond to her apology. I was lost in my own thoughts.

"Can you take me to room 345?" I asked as we came to main hall. "I would like to see my fiancée."

As she rolled me into his room, my heart began to do summersaults in my chest. Ronnie's face and majority of his upper body was wrapped and bandaged up. He looked something like a mummy.

"Thank you. May I have a few minutes alone with him?" I asked politely.

"Sure sweetie, just ring the bell when you're ready." She took one look at Ronnie and patted me on my shoulder before leaving. Seeing him laying there like that now put me in his shoes, two years ago.

"I love you so much baby, I am nothing without you. We need you to get better, our world depends on it. That's right I said we, Sariyah is here now babe and she's beautiful."

Beeeeep! An all too familiar alarm went off.

"Nooo Roonniee! Please don't do this babe, please don't stop fighting!"

Less than a minute later, the room was swarmed with a bunch of blue and white and I was rolled out in the hallway. As I sat in the middle of the hall, my nerves and emotions got the best of me. I bowed my head, said a prayer and cried until it felt like I stepped out of my body.

A pair of warm embracing hands engulfed my shoulders. When I looked up, I locked eyes with the warm pair of hazel brown eyes belonging to Dr. O'Neil. I don't know what it was but staring into his beautiful eyes seemed to soothe my aching heart. It was like his eyes danced with my soul to a slow melody.

"He's going to be alright," Bryan said, wrapping his large arms around my sore body.

"What went wrong Bryan? One second he was fine, I told him our daughter was here and then he flat lined,"

"Rondell is very fragile right now; the news of his first child being born probably made him very excited and overworked his weak heart. He's stable right now but I would suggest no more surprising news because I can't promise he'll recover."

I barely heard anything he said because I was lost in his arms; his grip was strong but humbling. I don't know why at a time like this I'd be feeling this way about my doctor. His cologne was scrambling my senses and causing me to tingle in places I shouldn't be. I reluctantly pulled myself out of his arms.

"Um, thank you Bryan. I promise no more shocking news,"

I guess he hadn't realized he'd been holding on to me either.

"Uh, it's nothing, just doing my job," he said, adjusting his clothes.

"If anything else happens, I'll let you know but for now I'm taking you back to your room."

I didn't object. I was physically drained and didn't mind getting some rest. When we reached my room I knew rest would be out of the question. Shadow was sitting near my bed. He looked like he'd seen better days. I felt his pain though, if not more. The love of his life and my only friend, my sister was gone. Just the thought of her made me tear up; life would never be the same.

"Do you feel like having company?" Bryan whispered in my ear.

"Yea, he's cool. Good night."

As Bryan shut the door, Shadow let out a soul clenching wail. "What am I going to do without her Tonya? She was my everything!"

I climbed into bed with tears rolling down my face.

"I don't know, but I do know that whoever was behind this will pay!" I screamed out.

Shadow's tears stopped and a sinister smile appeared. "Yo, you know whatever you have planned, I'm all in like a poker hand."

I laid back and let the wheels turn as plan vengeance formulated.

THIS GAME CALLED *Life*

CHAPTER SEVENTEEN

Time Doesn't Heal All

My stay in the hospital was supposed to last for only four days but the day before I was to be released, I spiked a 103.1 fever. After various test, I was diagnosed with endometritis. Bryan said it was an infection in the lining my uterus and that I shouldn't worry too much because it was common for women who've had a C-section. I say everything happens for a reason because I wasn't ready to leave the hospital anyway. Sariyah was still going to be in the hospital for another two weeks and now so was I.

I didn't mind the fact that Bryan came to check on me every day either. We had wonderful talks, even opened up about some of our life experiences. I found it odd that I was able to talk so freely with him and vice versa, in fact it was scary. I limited my contact with Ronnie as much as my heart could bare because I didn't want any repeats of the scare he gave me. The days I didn't see Ronnie, I would go sit with my babygirl.

One evening, I was singing to her and she turned her head in the direction of my voice. I looked into her tiny face and saw a miniature Alex looking back at me. It was then I decided that her name would no longer be Sariyah. The last two weeks flew by and it was almost time for me and Alexandria to go home and unfortunately, Ronnie was still unresponsive. It was decided that we would be leaving here without him and though it pained me, I knew he was in good hands.

I lay in bed, thinking about the days ahead of me when there was a knock on my room door.

"Come in." I knew it was Bryan. He'd been coming by every night at the same time for the past couple of weeks.

"Hello, beautiful," Bryan said as he entered.

"Hey, good looking," I responded.

This had become a little flirting game we played, after he walked in on me crying one night.

"So you're leaving tomorrow, excited?"

"Not really," I responded and looked away. I didn't want him to see the tears that built up every time I thought about going home without Ronnie

"Not really? Don't tell me you started liking the hospital food." Bryan joked, attempting to lift my spirits.

"No, that's one thing I can't wait to get away from," I said with a weak smile.

"There's that beautiful smile," he said, flashing a set of pearly whites of his own.

"You know the procedure, lay back and let me check your stitches. We should be able to get these out for you before you leave."

I was hesitant to lie back, not because I didn't trust him but because I didn't trust myself. The past couple of nights I found myself having lustful dreams about the doctor and we were taking a wild tumble on this hospital bed. The dream always started with him checking my stitches and then his hands would travel lower down into my panties.

He would use his masculine fingers to gently pry my legs open, putting little pressure as he fondled my precious button. While looking deep into my eyes, he'd pull his fingers gently out and suck my juices off each finger. Never taking his hazel eyes off mine, he'd begin lowering the bottom of the bed to be able to position himself better. The touch of his warm hands caused me to let out a moan and the pinch from him removing my stitches snapped me back to reality. I'd gotten caught up in my fantasy and forgot that Bryan was actually here in my room.

I prayed that he hadn't heard me but looking down at his confused face let me know I was praying on deaf ears.

"Is everything alright Tonya," he said, taking a seat next to me.

"Uh, yea, everything is good, just anticipating the trip going home." I lied.

"Oh ok, well your temperature is down, the infection seems to be gone, you're healing great, your stitches are out, so you're all set to leave tomorrow. If you ever need anything, here is my card...don't hesitate to call for whatever," he said, handing me his business card.

"I know I've said it a lot but I just want to thank you again for everything. You've been more than exceptional over these last few weeks."

"Like I've said, I'm just doing my job. Goodnight Tonya." He smiled and walked out the room. I breathed a sigh of relief, took one last look at his card before I tore it up and put it in the trash. A friendship outside of this hospital with Bryan would be nothing but trouble and that's trouble neither of us wanted. I rolled on my side, closed my eyes and resumed my dream about the handsome doctor.

BRYAN O'NEIL

Ronnie and I have been in the same circle for years. We used to all be best friends; me, him and Daryl. You could say that Ronnie and I were born with silver spoons in our mouths but Daryl lived a life of undercover struggle. He tried to conceal his misfortunes when around us but I could see right through his charade. I never said anything though because it wasn't my place, so I pretended I never noticed.

Ronnie and I both excelled in school, graduating a

year before time. We went to the same college, he took up business and I went into medical studies. A short time after graduation, Ronnie's parents were brutally murdered. Their deaths changed Ronnie, turned him into someone I no longer knew. While establishing his street crew, he asked me to be his second in command.

I tried to convince him that we were raised to stay out of the streets, so that we could live better lives than our parents. He told me that he was out for blood and no one could stop him. He gave me the option of riding with him or to go on living my life without him. I respectively declined his offer of the street life and hoped that he'd understand. He said he understood but that he had an empire to run and it would be best for me to act as if he never existed.

That was the last conversation I'd ever had with Ronnie. He went on to become a powerful and feared drug dealing, cold blooded, murdering lunatic that would take anyone down who threatened his stability. I on the other hand, finished medical school top of my class, completed my residency and now I am a qualified surgeon. I still live in the same neighborhood, just a few houses down from Ronnie. We see one another all the time but never acknowledge each other's presence. It's like he asked of me, *he never existed*.

From the first time I saw Tonya on the block with him, I thought she was the most beautiful young woman I'd ever laid eyes on. It wasn't only her physical beauty that had me stunned, her inner beauty shined brighter than any star. I could not and would not ever understand, for the life of me, why a woman of her stature would entertain the likes of a man like him. The night they were brought in and I heard the names, I quickly took the cases.

Being her doctor for the past couple of weeks gave me an opportunity that I wouldn't normally have gotten under any other circumstances. I was able to make a connection with her, something I am not suppose to do and never planned on doing but it was something about her that screamed, *I am different*. The more we talked, the more she opened up, the more I felt for her. As she told her story, she spoke with such confidence and strength but I could see the hurt and the pain in her eyes. As I reflected on our conversations, I said a silent prayer for her, asking God to protect and guide her. I went to check on her beau Mr. Jackson.

Opening his dressings, I could see that his wounds were healing nicely, no need for surgery.

"You're a lucky SOB, that woman you got is a keeper," I said to his unconscious body as my thoughts drifted back to Tonya.

"I-I-I know." I damn near fell over the stool when I heard him respond.

"Ronnie, if you can hear me I need you to move your hand." His hand moved. "Can you speak Ronnie? How are you feeling?"

"Bry-Bry-n?"

"Yes, it's me.

For the next several minutes, Ronnie and I went back and forth with him speaking a little more each time he tried. As he became more conscious he was able to speak easier and was squeezing my hand. I was so happy for him.

"Ronnie, how are you feeling," I asked him again.

"I-I-I'm not sure Bryan. I-I can't feel my legs, why can't I feel my legs Bryan?" Ronnie yelled in desperation. His heart rate started to increase.

"I don't know Ronnie but I will find out. Please calm down."

I walked out to the nurses' station and paged the neurologist. Four hours later, Ronnie was diagnosed with temporary paralysis and because I chose the shorter straw, I had to be the bearer of bad news.

"Hey Ronnie," I said, still trying to figure out the right words to say without setting him off.

He was wide awake now. "Cut the bullshit Bryan and give it to me straight, will I ever walk again?"

"Here it is, yes you will walk again but I can't give you a timeframe,"

"What the fuck do you mean you can't give me a timeframe?"

"I mean exactly what I said, I can't give you a timeframe. If you want to walk again, that's entirely on you."

"Ok I hear you. So, how is Tonya? Is my daughter ok?"

"They're both fine, they're being released as we speak."

"Released? Why am I not being released with them? I want to be released too!"

"I wish it was that simple Ronnie but I am afraid that can't happen. You've just awakened from being in a coma and have just received the paralysis diagnosis. You will not be released several weeks. Your release will be contingent on how your body reacts to physical therapy."

"I don't know what the hell you're talking about but I know that I can sign out of here on my own free will. So, take your happy go lucky ass to the front desk and get my fucking release papers before I get upset."

I tried to be professional but this dude wanted to get ignorant with me and I lost my cool.

"I don't know who the fuck you think you're talking to but you better check yourself nigga. We are from the same hood with the same background or did you forget? Don't let this white coat fool you!"

Once I was done venting, Ronnie wasn't the only one surprised. I hadn't stepped out of my character in a long time but that's what happens when people take you there and I wasn't the least bit apologetic.

"Whoa, Nigga! I think it's you that must've forgot who the fuck you're talking too but I will let this one slide because I did come off crazy. For future reference, don't ever come out the side of your face like that to me again or those will be the last words you'll ever speak. Now get the fuck out my face and get my fucking papers!"

I wanted to give him an overdose of morphine in his IV but decided the scumbag wasn't worth everything I worked so hard to obtain.

TONYA

Wiping the sleep out my eyes, I dragged myself out the bed. I wasn't really prepared to leave Ronnie here but I had no choice, today was the day I went home with my daughter, Alexandria. Two hours later there was a knock on my door. It was Nurse Joyce with my discharge papers.

"Good morning Tonya. Ready to get out of here?"

"Morning Joyce, I'm as ready as I'll ever be at this point."

Joyce handed me the papers and I reluctantly signed them.

"Good luck with that precious little girl, Tonya and may God bless you both."

"Thank you Joyce and good luck with whatever decision you and your daughter come to."

As soon as she left, I took a shower and mentally prepared myself for the start of my future. An hour later I was sitting outside in a wheelchair with Ms. Estelle, watching Shadow struggle to put Alexandria's car seat in the car properly.

"You be sure to call me Tonya, if either of you ever need anything," Ms. Estelle said, using my back as support while she wrote down her information. "I don't care what time it is, day or night."

"Aw, thank you Ms. Estelle, that means a lot to me and I will definitely keep in touch," I said as Shadow rolled me to the passenger's side. He helped me in and made sure both me and Alexandria were secure.

"Ok sis, where are we off to? Home?"

"Na, I'm not ready to go home yet," I sighed. "Can we go to Babies R' Us? There's some things I still need to get." After two hours in Babies R' Us and a stop at Pathmark, we finally made it home. I grabbed a couple of the bags from the backseat and headed towards the door as Shadow gathered Alexandria from the car. As I put the key in the door, a shadowy figure moved fast past the large window in the living room.

"What the fuck was that?" I yelled, instinctively reaching inside my bag for my new 9mm upgrade I brought a few weeks back. Before I could look over my shoulder in Shadow's direction, he was already standing beside me with his customized .380 locked, loaded and fixed on the door.

"Take the baby and go back to the car sis! I got this! Niggas done fucked with the wrong one!" Shadow said, pushing me back toward the car but never taking his eyes of the door.

"Na bro, you're not going in there by yourself," I said pushing against him, trying to get to the door.

"Take your ass back to the car with my niece, now Tonya!" he said, pushing me rather hard this time.

After a push like that I didn't object. I hurried back to the car, jumped in the driver's seat and locked the doors. I watched Shadow creep in the house and as soon as he turned in the direction of the living room, the door slammed shut.

"Shaadoooww ...nooooo!" I screamed.

I jumped out the car and ran toward the house with

my gun drawn. I kicked the front door in, "Shadow!" I yelled, stepping into the apartment.

Suddenly the lights flicked on and I slightly tripped on something. When I looked down, Shadow was sprawled out behind the door. "Shadow?" I called out to him while bending down to check for his pulse.

"He'll be just fine," a raspy. masculine voice said from behind me. I turned toward the voice with the quickness of a cheetah and the aim of a marksman. One thing Ronnie taught me was to shoot first and ask questions later and that was my intentions, until I was face to face with my home's invader.

All the air evaporated from my lungs and my knees became weaker than a cooked noodle. I couldn't believe that I was looking into the face of my love. The last time I'd seen him was four days ago and he was in a coma and unresponsive but now here he sat on this motorized scooter, gazing at me.

"I don't understand Ronnie, h-how? W-w-hen?"

I was so overwhelmed with emotion, I couldn't form a sentence.

"Why are you in a wheelchair? What happened to Shadow? What did you do to him?" My mouth was moving a mile a minute.

"Slow down Babygirl, one question at a time. Now I'm in this wheelchair because I'm temporarily paralyzed and as far as Shadow goes, I hit him with the umbrella holder."

"What? Why would you do that?"

"I had to do something Tonya! That's my brother and

I know how his mind operates. He would've shot me on site! No questions asked."

"This is crazy Ronnie, what are you doing home? When were you released from the hospital?"

"It's a long story but I'm just glad to be home. Where is my daughter? I want to see her."

"Oh shit!"

I had left and forgotten Alexandria in the car during the chaos. I dashed out of the house, unlocked the car and picked up my crying babygirl. Ronnie rolled outside with a staggering Shadow following close behind.

"Is that her?"

I slowly approached them as Alexandria was starting to calm down.

"Ronnie this is our daughter, Alexandria Lanett Jackson," I said, resting our creation in Ronnie's outstretched arms.

RONNIE

"Alexandria! What made you choose that name?"

I wasn't feeling the fact that my daughter was named after that bitch. I knew they were close and all that but we had a name picked out already, so why change it especially to that hoe's name. Tonya had this foul look on her face.

"What! How could you even ask a question like that?" she yelled and snatched Alexandria away from me and stormed into the house. Even Shadow was staring at me like I cursed his grandmother.

"What the fuck is wrong with y'all?"

I looked around at their sour faces.

"Alex is gone, bro," Shadow said, breaking down into tears and following Tonya inside.

Oh shit! I hadn't really remembered much until then and that's when it all came flashing back, they now knew Alex was dead too. It was time for some damage control.

"Damn babe! I didn't remember until just now. I'm so sorry. We're going to find out who did this," I said, rolling into the house.

About a week before Alex's body was discovered, I received a package at one of my traps. After inspecting the package and finding no return information, I was cynical about opening it so I left it on my desk and went to lunch. When I came back, looking at the box just sitting there became agitating and I finally gave in and opened it.

My stomach felt like it turned inside out and knotted itself into a thousand bows. I threw up majority of my lunch when I saw the contents inside—three fingers, two toes and a tennis bracelet. The body parts, I immediately knew belonged to Alex because the tennis bracelet taped to them was the same one that Shadow had given her recently. In my heart, I knew Alex was dead and even though I was pissed at her for burning me, I would've never harmed her because I knew how much she meant to Tonya. I started secretly combing the streets looking for any information leading to her disappearance but nobody knew or heard anything. With nothing coming from the streets, I decided that it was time to tell my brother about the package I received but I was too late...

When Shadow called that night, while we were on our way home from dinner and told us about the suitcase containing Alex's body, it confirmed her death. I was infuriated. Somebody had violated in the worse way and once I found out who it was, they would pay the same ultimate price.

"Ronnie?" Tonya's chants snatched me back to reality. "Ronnie, are you okay? Thought we'd lost you there for a second," she said, rubbing my face.

"I'm more than ok. How could I not be okay with this precious little girl in my arms?" I gestured for Tonya to come to me. "I want to thank you for this priceless gift of life that we created out of love."

I pulled her down for a sweet passionate kiss that made her knees quiver. I loved the fact that I could still make her knees buckle with just a simple touch. Shadow drank a few with me and then cried himself to sleep on the couch. I felt bad for my brother, he really did love Alex. I couldn't even imagine how I'd be if someone killed the love of my life. While Tonya prepared dinner, I laid Alexandria down and then snuck into my office to make a few phone calls.

CHAPTER EIGHTEEN

Nothing is Ever What It Appears To Be

CANDIE

The sudden loud ringing of my house phone startled me as I was preparing my water for a relaxing soak in a bubble filled tub. *Damn, who the hell could this be messing up my flow*, I wondered as dashed to my room. My mood completely changed once I saw Tonya's name on the caller ID, I hadn't seen nor spoken to her since her court appearance. After everyone disbursed, I headed out of town to handle some personal business. A week into my trip I got a phone call from my daughter Katrina, telling me that Ronnie and Tonya had gotten into a near fatal accident and were touch and go. I flew back that same day and even though I wanted to see Ronnie bad, I couldn't stomach seeing him in that condition.

"Hey mamas, congratulations on the birth of that beautiful princess. I know she's gorgeous."

"What's good ma?" The sound of his deep and sexy raspy voice sent spine tingling chills all over my body.

"Oh Ronnie, you don't know how good it is to hear your voice right now. Are you okay? How are you feeling?"

"I could be doing a lot better ma, they got your man locked down in this wheelchair but I'm a solider so I'll be good. How is my little man doing? Getting big I know."

"We've been doing well. He's been kicking up a storm and I've been getting those Braxton Hicks contractions lately. It's hard to believe that he'll be here in a few weeks."

"Yea, I can't wait! When are you coming home ma?"

"I don't know babe but soon, I'll be home soon."

"Look I want to see you; can we link up in an hour at the spot?"

"I don't know Ronnie. What will Tonya say about you wanting to leave out?"

"Don't worry about Tonya, I'll handle her, now are you coming or not?"

"Yes babe, I'll see you in an hour."

"Iight ma, see you soon, I love you."

"I love you too," I said hanging up the phone.

I wonder would he still love me if he knew who and

what I was about. Could he still love me if he knew I was a thirty-six year old TRAPSTER with a daughter a year younger than him and not a twenty seven year old grad student working her way through college. I'd been in the game of trapping dudes for twenty one years. I began shortly after I had Katrina at the tender age of fifteen. I was a young mom with nothing—no home, no money, no food. The only time we had shelter were the nights I could afford train fare, other than that, Central Park was our home.

By the time Katrina was five months old, I got tired of the bullshit. One night I was on the Number Two train riding from Flatbush Ave in Brooklyn to 241st Street in the Bronx. As I looked into the face of my sleeping angel, the faces of her bastard father and my junkie mother appeared. I thought back on her last words to me, before she sold me to fuck that nigga for an eighth of that new rock form of cocaine.

"Its ok baby," she said, "the sooner you accept that all you'll ever be good for is lying on your back and spreading those legs just like your mama, the better off you'll be. You'll understand the power of your twat one day and when you do, it'll become your personal goldmine."

That was the last time I saw her alive. She overdosed that night on that corner. As the train was approaching 125th Street, I made a decision that would change our lives forever. Back then Harlem had been rocked by the *crack epidemic*. Crack was a solid, smokeable, more potent form of cocaine. The streets of Harlem were now overpopulated with crackheads and derelicts. I wrapped

Katrina up with all my valuables secretly hidden in her pants and I walked the streets looking for any drug dealer who seemed like he was making big money. By the time I reached 125th and Park Ave, I was ready to say forget it, then a beeping horn startled me.

"Hey sexy, where you going this time of night?"

I started to walk away when my mother's words replayed, "*You'll understand the power of your twat one day and when you do, it'll become your personal goldmine*".

"From the looks of it, with you," I smirked and walked toward the car.

"Umph, sounds about right to me. Get your fine ass in this car. Deshawn turned out to be a nice guy. He paid me $80, bought KFC for me and formula for Katrina. He paid the room up for a week so we'd have somewhere to sleep. With a full belly for the first time in weeks, Katrina bathed and fed, a warm bed to sleep in and money in my pockets, I slept peacefully.

After a week of sucking and fucking, I saved up over $500 and it was time to move on. I was laying in bed contemplating my next moves when the room door opened.

"You scared the shit out of me Deshawn, what are you doing here?"

"I came to offer you a business proposition. How would you like to work for me?" he said, taking a seat at the table.

"Work for you how? You know I ain't selling no drugs," I said, sitting up, eager to hear what he was offering.

"No, of course I don't want you selling drugs. I have another business that I own. I run an escort business. I know that you would be a valuable asset to my business. What you think about that?"

"What do I think about that? I think you're a pimp trying to recruit me"

"I ain't no pimp, I'm a Proper Instructor Making Paper. I'm all about making money; you wouldn't be doing anything you weren't comfortable with. I would never have you walking the streets. You'd always have money, food, clothes and shelter and before you ask, I have an in-house sitter for the children."

"Children?"

"Yes children. Some of my employees are mothers."

After a few moments of weighing my other options and realizing I had none, I agreed.

We packed up that night and moved in the Trappers House. Everything was as he said it would be—I started making money immediately. A few years into the game, I was straightening up his office and stumbled upon his record book. Being nosy I opened the book, flipped through it until I found my name. I was surprised how organized he was, there were detailed entries for every customer I ever had from my first day working. At first glance I was hyped, I had the most bookings and requests. That arrogance quickly turned to anger when I looked at the columns titled Intake and Payout. Every transaction he charged $175 per client but was only paying me $85. Even though I was pissed, I wouldn't let it show; no time to get angry but I would definitely get even. I made photocopies of my client list, which contained their names, addresses and numbers. I grabbed Katrina, bagged all my shit and drove off in my Honda Accord.

That day I went into business for myself and have been ever since. My vibrating cell phone brought me back to the present day.

"Hey babe, so where you able to get out?"

"Yea, I'm here already, where are you?"

"Damn you must really miss me, you all early and ish!" I chuckled into the phone as I rolled up my lace stockings.

"Early? Girl I've been here for over forty-five minutes, you're late!"

I looked at the clock on my wall, and I damn sure was forty-five minutes late.

"I'm sorry baby, I got caught up getting sexy for you. I'll be there in less than fifteen."

"Alright Ma, hurry up," he said, hanging up the phone. I looked in mirror one last time, seven months pregnant and looking great. I carried mostly in my back so I didn't have much of a belly. I just really started to show a few weeks ago. One quick look at my watch, I snatched my keys off the night stand and headed out the door.

RONNIE

After a brief argument with Tonya, I finally got her to understand that I'd been off the block for while and that it was necessary for me to show my face. She didn't like it but she knew I had to check on things in person. As soon as we turned the corner, I gave Shadow the address to the hotel. I felt semi-bad for lying to Tonya because I really did love her but I loved Candie too. I know we promised Tonya a few months ago that our relationship would remain platonic but there was no way to deny our chemistry. We even signed a fake contract, just something to keep Tonya happy but truth be told, I was fucking Candie every night after Tonya fell asleep. Sometimes I would fuck them both in the same night. What can I say, when you got it like that you got it! And I definitely had it.

I looked at my watch. *Damn I hope she hurry up.* I pulled out blunt, sparked it, and got my mind right. Twenty minutes later there was a light tap on the door.

I opened the door and in stepped Tonya.

"W-w-what are you doing here Tonya?" I asked as she rushed in past me.

"What the fuck are you doing here Ronnie? Who the fuck you got in here with you?"

"Ain't nobody fucking here, I have a meeting in a few! Now I'm not going to ask you again, what the hell are you doing here and where is Alexandria?"

I couldn't believe this shit, what the fuck was she doing here. I prayed to God that Candie didn't show up right now.

"I had a gut feeling that you were lying about going to the block so I followed you. Can you imagine my surprise to follow you to a fucking hotel! Like for real

Ronnie, are you fucking serious! I just gave birth to your daughter and this is the best you got for me."

"I just told your ass that I have a meeting here in a few. You need to take yourself and my daughter home!" I screamed at her. "Fuck you following me for Inspector Gadget? I'm a grown ass man!"

"I don't believe you Ronnie," she said, not budging.

"You don't believe me, then call Shadow and ask him."

She wasted no time dialing his number. I wasn't worried though, I knew my brother would hold me down. By the apologetic look on her face, I knew that he'd confirmed my story.

"I'll see your ass at home," I said, dismissing her.

After she left, I sparked a blunt and called Candie. She didn't answer. I called a few more times, still no answer. She had ten minutes to show up or I was out and she would hear about it later. I smoked two more blunts waiting for her. I must've drifted off to sleep. Next thing I knew I was waking up…it was 5:00 a.m. After taking a piss, I checked my phone. The only missed calls and texts were from Tonya asking me to come home—nothing from Candie. To say I was disappointed would be an understatement. I called Shadow to come pick me up. He got there around 6 a.m. He helped me get in the house about a half an hour later and I told him I could handle it from there. When I reached the living room I saw a pallet of pillows and a blankets on the couch. Deciding not to argue with her, I laid down and attempted to call Candie one more time.

The phone was answered on the fifth ring. "Yo what happened to you last night," I whispered in the receiver.

"Who the fuck is this?" a dude's voice shouted through the phone.

"Who the fuck is this and what the fuck you doing with my baby mom's phone?"

"Nigga, this is my bitch's phone! Who the fuck is this? Is this that bitch ass nigga Ronnie?"

"I don't think you know who you're fucking with my man, that's a war you want no part of! Now where the fuck is Candie?"

"She busy nigga!"

"Busy doing what nigga? Put her on the fucking phone! NOW!"

Click. That bitch nigga hung the phone up on me. I called back like ten times…no one answer. So that hoe want to play a nigga! After all that I sacrificed for her. As I sat there and thought of her being with the next dude, tears started falling—tears of hurt, confusion and anger.

COMING SOON!!!

I would like to thank you all for the continuous love and support. Without y'all there is no me. *This Game Called Life* is my first novel and it's been by far the hardest story to tell. I started writing a story similar to TGCL when I was in the seventh grade, but with no real life experience I was unable to develop the story I wanted to tell. Now, years later I've seen, heard and done things that most average fifty year old people haven't even thought of. Thus giving me the *juice* necessary to tell you this heart-breaking tale of Tonya's life.

I hope by the end of this trilogy, I will have opened someone's eyes to the signs of child abuse, given light to the possible outcomes of an abused child's life after it's all said and done or even encouraged a child or teen to speak out against their abuser(s).

To my parent readers; There are too many Tonya's in the world. If we'd just pay a little more attention to our children, listen to them when they speak, no matter how outrageous they may sound and talk to them even if we're the only one talking, stories like Tonya's can be PREVENTED. If God forbid something like this happens to your child, we as parents need to stop enforcing that old saying, *What goes on in the house stays in the house* upon our children. Abused children need as much support as possible, so encourage your children to speak out…you may just be saving their lives.

- Marie A. Norfleet

For the latest updates, upcoming book releases from G Street Chronicles visit www.gstreetchronicles.com

If you would like to interact with Marie A. Norfleet personally, join her on Facebook: http://www.facebook.com/authormarien or on Twitter: @authormarien